I0714711

BEAST

A PROTECTOR EMOTIONAL SCARS DARK MAFIA ROMANCE

STRUCK IN LOVE
BOOK THREE

CHIQUITA DENNIE

304 PUBLISHING COMPANY

Copyright@2017 Chiquita Dennie
Published by 304 Publishing Company

All Rights Reserved. Except for use in any review, no portion of this book may be performed, reproduced, published, sold or distributed by any means, or quoted in any medium. Including on any website, without prior written consent from the owner.

This is a work of fiction. Names, characters, places and incidents are either the product of the author's imagination or are used fictitiously, and any resemblance to actual persons, living or dead, business establishments, events or locales is entirely coincidental.

For questions and comments about this book, please contact 304 Publishing Company.

Visit the official website at www.chiquitadennie.com

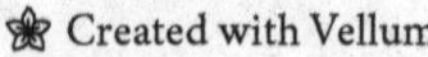 Created with Vellum

LATEST RELEASES

*L*atest Releases from Chiquita Dennie
The Early Years-A Prequel Short Story
Antonio and Sabrina: Struck in Love 1, 2, 3,4,5
Heart of Stone, Book 1 (Emery & Jackson)
Heart Of Stone Book 1.5 Emery &Jackson A Valentine's Day Short
Janice and Carlo: Captivated By His Love
Heart of Stone, Book 2 (Jordan and Damon)
Temptation
Heart of Stone, Book 3 (Angela and Brent)
Cocky Catcher
Bossy Billionaire
Bottoms Up Heart of Stone, Book 3.5(Jessica and Joseph Short
Love Shorts: A Collection of Short Stories
Joaquin Fuertes (The Fuertes Cartel Book 1)
Exposed (Salvation Society Novel)
Joaquin Fuertes (The Fuertes Cartel Book 2)
Refuel (A Driven World Novel)

Pressure (A Driven World Novel)
Until Serena (HEA World Novel)
Antonio and Sabrina: Struck in Love 5
Red Light District (A Fantasy Romance Short)
Heart of Stone, Book 4 (Jessica and Joseph)
She's All I Need
Something Gained (A Romantic Comedy)
Upcoming Releases (2022/2023):
Summer Break Series 1-3
Small Town Series 1-4
Dare To Love

I want to thank first and foremost God for giving me the strength to keep pursuing my dreams and goals. My mom and big brother. Niece and nephew, and to all of my cousins. Especially a huge thanks to my family in heaven Grandmother, Aunt, Father. Always with me no matter where I go and everything you've taught me has made me a better person.

AUTHOR INSPIRATION

"*Never allow anyone to steal your joy. It doesn't matter how many times someone says you can't do something. Invest in yourself—even if it's just writing down what your goals and plans are. Starting small can lead to bigger things.*"

—Chiquita Dennie

DISCLAIMER

This work of fiction contains strong language and explicit sexual content and is only intended for mature readers. This story may contain unconventional situations, language, and sexual encounters that may offend some readers. If you're looking for sweet, fluffy romance, I would recommend another book. This book is for mature readers (18+).

INTRODUCTION

A fun fact is that Antonio and Sabrina: Struck In Love Series is actually based on a screenplay I wrote right after college, getting my first taste of Hollywood. This story will cause you to scream, yell, laugh, and probably cry. Grab some wine and get ready for more spicy, sinful, sexy fun with Antonio, Sabrina, Carlo, and sassy Janice.

Are you signed up for my newsletter?

Join today and find out all the latest in new releases, contests, giveaways, sneak peeks and more.

www.chiquitadennie.com

SYNOPSIS

*I*s the past ever really in the past?

Antonio:

Being the Don of the De Luca Cartel was supposed to be my dream come true.

It was my birth right, what I have been working for.

With that title comes more responsibility and new threats that have me wondering if this is worth it.

Sabrina:

This should be the happiest time of my life.

I'm wildly in love, but I'm not sure that I can keep living like this.

All of that danger that I found so intriguing about Antonio and his world is now a threat to me and my family.

After coming to terms with the past, I'm wondering if this is the wake-up call that I needed.

Maybe it's time to walk away from Antonio.

Even if it means breaking my heart in the process.

Will these two be able to fight off the enemies from

their past and get the love story they both so desperately want?

CHAPTER ONE

SABRINA

One year later in Italy.

I was sitting in our baby boy's nursery, breast-feeding a seven-pound, five-ounce, cinnamon skin-toned, blue-eyed baby boy who I named him AJ—short for Antonio De Luca Jr.

I still couldn't believe how time had passed, and no one had any luck in finding me.

Dealing with recurring nightmares of that tragic night when Alex kidnapped me from outside my apartment, I was scared for not only my life but my child's as well. I couldn't help but think I should have fought harder.

Thinking back a few weeks ago, I decided to give into Alex's demands with seducing him. I prayed he'd fall for my act. At the last minute, when it came down to it, I couldn't betray Antonio and the love we created together. Alex made it difficult with his little kisses and touches every other minute, I wanted to throw up at his touch.

He made my skin crawl. Rather than dealing with another night of torture, I pretended to be in another dream world. That Alex was Antonio. Pretending made my days go by faster. Having our son look exactly like his father was a bonus. Alex couldn't stand AJ. I kept him always locked in his room to keep him safe. Camilla popped by every few days with updates from my family's pursuit of finding me.

"Are you coming to bed, Bri?" Alex inquired.

Smiling down at AJ, I kissed his forehead, snuggled up to his cheek, and prayed for another night of peace.

"I'll be there in a minute, Alex," I replied.

Alex looked at me lovingly, reminiscent of a time back when we were in love. Having a baby by another man was hurtful, slowly turning Alex cold, which was disheartening not only toward me, but my baby as well.

Alex hadn't seen his so-called child in almost a year. Sharon, the woman he cheated on me with, stopped taking his calls almost a year ago. She went back and forth with him in court and finally came to realize it wasn't his kid. He still had love for the child he helped raise. He worked with Camilla to break Antonio and me up. They both plotted to kill Antonio while Camilla inherited his family's fortune and control of the cartel business.

It didn't help that Antonio couldn't stand Camilla after he found out about her working with Alfredo shooting Antonio. He figured it was best to cut all communications off with Sharon until the dust cleared. After not responding for a month, he flew back to the States. Learning from his mother that Sharon up and remarried and moved away, left him livid and bitter toward her. She turned out to be a home wrecker that broke up his relationship with me. He knew deep down that I hated him. But I just needed a little time to learn to love him like I used to, kill him, and then escape.

"Don't keep me waiting, baby," Alex says impatiently.

He walked into the jungle-themed nursery and kissed

me on the cheek. I tensed up at the kiss, and he felt me pull away abruptly.

"I won't," I replied.

AJ fussed in my arms. He always seemed to get fussy when Alex came around. I hoped Alex wouldn't put up a fight tonight, or maybe I could pretend I was too exhausted for sex. It had been nine months since I had AJ and over a year since my kidnapping. The only type of physical intimacy I'd allowed so far was hugging and holding hands. I was already a few months along in my pregnancy the night I was taken from my home.

All the nights I let him cuddle and hold me in bed at night had his dick hard throughout the entire night. Only thing I did to please him was a hand job. Back when we were together, oral sex was always a favorite of us both. I couldn't even fathom doing something like that now. In the words of my friend Janice, "I'd rather become a nun and give up sex for the rest of my life before I stoop that low on the totem pole."

"I'm right behind you," I muttered.

Alex walked out as I finally got AJ to calm down. A lone tear rolled down my cheek. Looking at our son made me think about his father and what he'd been dealing with for the past year. Would he still love me after all this time?

"What if he's married to someone else?" I somberly wondered to myself.

Taking in all his features, I stood and watched as he slept, realizing the love I shared with Antonio helped to create a beautiful baby boy with dark, curly hair, deep, ocean-blue eyes like his father, a small button nose like me, and skin the color of cinnamon.

I bent down and kissed him on the forehead, turned around, and walked out. Walking toward the bedroom that

I shared with Alex, I hesitated for a moment and heard Alex talking to someone on the phone.

"Do you have any updates?"

"We can't stay locked away here forever," Alex whispered into the phone. "I can feel her wanting to run again."

I inched the door slightly open and saw Alex's back turned away from me.

"Listen, Camilla, you hiding out from him won't get anything solved. At some point, he'll figure it out that we kidnapped her. Has he said anything about the baby?" Alex asked.

Alex turned around just as I came further into the room. He hung up the phone hurriedly.

"Who were you talking with?" I asked.

"It doesn't concern you, babe," Alex answered. I watched as he placed his phone on the charger and locked in the cabinet. He placed the key around his neck. Grabbing some pajamas, he headed to take a shower and change for bed.

"I need to get out of here."

I watched as Alex went into the bathroom and started the shower, making sure I had enough time to get to his phone and make a call.

I waited five minutes as he turned the radio on, and music floated out of the en suite.

"Bri Bri, you should join me. The water feels good," Alex yelled.

I cringed at the thought of Alex touching me and sleeping in the same bed as him every night. Luckily, I'd been able to avoid him while I was pregnant. Now that I'd healed, my plan to escape may include sleeping with him.

"I already showered."

Walking over to the cabinet, I tried to open it with a hard jerk. It didn't work. Looking around for what else I could use, I came up empty. All the knives were taken away after I tried stabbing Alex a few months back during what he described as a romantic, candlelight dinner for two.

"Fuck…"

The water in the bathroom turned off. I jumped to place everything back. I took off my clothes and walked over to the bed, turning the light off, so Alex didn't notice anything moved.

"Bri, tomorrow we should take Alex Jr. to the park," Alex said.

Sighing in frustration, I turned the light back on as Alex dried off and put his boxers and pajama pants on.

"His name is Antonio De Luca Jr. Not Alex."

Staring into his eyes for any hesitation or blowback from my response, Alex walked closer with a look of anguish etched across his face.

"My son won't carry that thug's name. Do you hear me?" Alex demanded.

Pulling me by the bottom of the chin and squeezing tight, he bent down and kissed me. I tried to move out of the way of his kiss, but he only squeezed tighter.

"Alex, you're hurting me," I pleaded.

"Then do as I say."

Glancing at the key around his neck, I thought about my son and getting out of the situation I'd been stuck in for a year. Knowing the only way to get out was by agreeing to Alex's demands, I replied, "Okay. We can call him Alex Jr."

Alex smiled and kissed me again. He let go and touched my cheek to see if he left a bruise.

"Don't worry, I didn't leave a mark on that pretty face of yours," Alex answered.

Alex walked to the other side of the bed, pulled the

covers back, and lay down. He pulled me into his arms and kissed my forehead.

"You should be completely healed by now, baby. It's time," Alex said.

I looked away, and a tear formed. Not wanting Alex to question anything, I quickly wiped it away.

"Not tonight, Alex. I'm exhausted from taking care of AJ," I answered. I yawned and hugged Alex as a way to distract him from the conversation of sex. "I think he'd like the park actually," I blurted out.

"I think so too. I'll make arrangements in the morning before my flight," Alex answered.

"Where are you going?" I inquired.

"I have business to take care of, nothing that concerns you. Now time for bed," Alex replied.

Alex closed his eyes and ran his hand down my back, caressing my shoulders. I let Alex do as he pleased for the time being until I could get the key and leave.

I drifted off to my happy place, dreaming of being in Antonio's arms.

"Baby, I want you out of that dress."

Antonio kissed my shoulder, slowly sliding the strap off.

"Tony, I'm watching this show. You promised to watch it with me," I moaned.

He cupped my breasts, kneading my right, then left, nipple.

"Would you prefer I stop, Bella?" he whispered and licked the side of my ear, nibbling right on the edge.

I arched into him and closed my eyes. The strain in my pussy was overwhelming.

"Huh?" I panted as the wetness between my legs seeped through my panties.

Antonio continued kissing me on my neck, then my cheeks.

"Baby, did I cause this?"

"Yes…" I strained with a sharp intake of breath.

I moved to Antonio and licked his bottom lip.

"Mmmmhhhh," Antonio groaned.

Suddenly, he pulled his hand out of my panties and turned to the TV.

"Actually, we should finish this later."

"What!"

"Didn't you say that you wanted to see this show on Showtime. The Chi from Lena White."

"What the fuck, Tony! You can't leave me like this."

I placed one finger inside and felt my wetness. Slowly moving my finger in and out, I felt my peak getting near. I sped up.

Feeling my body being shaken, I jumped up frantically.

"Sabrina, Sabrina? Wake up," Alex grumbled.

Looking around the room, I lowered my head in disappointment that I was still in Italy and not home with Antonio and our baby.

Antonio Jr was crying from the next room.

"I need to get a few things lined up before my flight. Alex Jr is crying. Try to get yourself together and meet me downstairs for breakfast," Alex demanded.

Slowly getting out of bed and grabbing my robe, I walked toward the door. Alex grabbed me forcefully by the arm.

"What the hell, Alex?" I shouted.

"Next time, try not to call out another man's name in my presence. Or I won't be so forgiving," Alex told me angrily.

Alex let my arm go, and I rubbed the pain away, nodding my head in agreement. I watched as he walked out and went downstairs. Then I approached Antonio Jr's room.

I walked into his room, and his crying got louder.

"Hey, Momma's baby."

I picked him up and patted his back to try to calm him down.

AJ's cries turned into whimpering.

"Momma's working on getting us out of here, I promise. Daddy can't wait to see you," I stated.

I kissed his cheek and forehead. Grabbing his favorite blanket, I walked into his bathroom and started the water in the tub for his morning bath.

I went to the monitor on the small side table and called for the in-house nurse.

"Buongiorno, Sabrina," Valentina stated.

"Buongiorno, Valentina. Can you come upstairs please with a bottle for AJ?" I asked.

"Of course, anything for my little bambini."

Pulling AJ's pajamas off and smiling at him, he sat back and giggled.

"You are so cute. Give me a kiss." I placed two kisses on each of his cheeks as he continued giggling.

Valentina walked into the nursery with a baby bottle.

"Here you go, Sabrina."

After Valentina passed his bottle of milk and caressed his cheek, I snuggled him into my arms and placed small kisses on his fingers and toes. Watching as he held the bottle with both hands and knowing Antonio had missed the most important moments of his son's life, made me even more pissed off at Alex and that bitch Camilla for plotting to keep Antonio and me away from each other.

"Can you check the water for me and make sure it's not too hot?"

"Sure, do you have any plans today?" Valentina replied and walked into the bathroom.

"I do, actually. Alex is taking us to the park."

I watched as Valentina stepped all the way into the bathroom. Placing AJ down on the bed and taking the bottle out of his mouth, he started to cry again.

"Did you see Alex leave yet?"

"Yes, he left in one car and said he'd be back before his flight. He just had a quick errand to run."

Glancing at the lamp on the side table, I knew this was my chance. I grabbed the lamp and watched as Valentina bent down closer to check the water.

I wrapped the cord around my hand and glanced over at AJ one more time before making the final decision.

CHAPTER TWO

ANTONIO

I'd been counting down the days since my love had been missing. Everyone kept saying she left me. I hadn't slept, eaten, or been the same since. My entire world up and changed when they told me she was gone. I knew it wasn't true. Camilla disappeared as well after we found out she'd been working with my Uncle Alfredo.

"Tony… it wasn't me," Spencer pleaded.

I kept replaying our last conversation at the restaurant. We put our pasts behind us and wanted to start over. Fuck, whatever my family said, Sabrina was mine.

I stood with my shirt splattered with blood from killing two more people in the warehouse involved in my uncle's scheme. "I have no doubt that you're not involved. But see, the problem is that you've been pissing me off from the start. You're always in the way of what we had going on," I spat.

Spencer cried as another blow landed to his stomach.

"Please… I can help you find her," Spencer cried out.

My phone rang. Carlo's name flashed across the screen.

Since everything went down with Sabrina, I'd avoided everyone, including my best friend.

Turning the phone off, I went back to torturing Spencer. Picking up the knife from the table, I smiled at the sharp blade.

"Hold him still," I told Sonny.

Spencer shook, pissing his pants.

"You can't do this. Please, I can help you," Spencer cried out.

As I reached Spencer and held the knife to his throat, Carlo and Bruno ran inside.

"Tony, drop the knife," Carlo demanded.

Bruno walked toward Spencer as Carlo tried to distract me.

"You can't kill him. He's not a part of our world," Carlo demanded.

"I'm the Don, brother, and I can do anything I want. Besides, I have no heart anymore. I feel nothing without her here next to me. The world would be better off without him here," I replied.

Carlo could tell I'd gone to a dark place. Without Sabrina here, and the cartel locked in a war with the Russians over Vlad's killing, I needed to get my emotions back in control.

"Carlo, you know me better than anyone. Tell me why I should spare this conniving bastard's life," I asked.

"He's not worth it, and at the end of the day, he works at a very high-profile company. Someone's bound to miss him. We don't need that kind of attention around us," Carlo replied.

Spencer's breathing evened out, and he shook his head in agreement with Carlo. Something told me I shouldn't trust him.

"Did you have anything to do with Sabrina's disappearance?" I asked.

"I swear to you I didn't. I loved her just as much as you," he answered.

I laughed at his acknowledgment of love, then plunged the knife deep into his heart.

"Antonio… arghhh!" Spencer bellowed.

Carlo and Bruno both looked at me in shock for killing Spencer. I had no remorse. He'd done nothing but try to influence Sabrina to stay away from me.

"Antonio," Carlo called out.

"I'm not Antonio, call me Capo. Anything or anyone that stands in the way of me getting my Bella back, will deal with Capo from here on out. Is that understood?"

CHAPTER THREE

BRUNO

Watching my little brother go through stages of becoming someone he wasn't had me feeling sorry for the poor guys who got in his way. We burned down homes, churches, and businesses to find out any information on Sabrina's whereabouts. Running my hands over my beard was a habit I'd picked up since I grew it out. It helped my thought process when I became frustrated with a situation.

"I hate to say it, Pops, but we need to find her and fast. He's losing his mind."

My father waved off the suggestion.

"He's fine. We didn't need her involved in cartel business; that little whore was just a distraction. First and foremost, La Famiglia."

"What do you have against the girl? Let's be honest. I wouldn't pass up the chance to sleep with her. Marry... probably not, but good pussy comes a dime a dozen."

Carlo and Antonio walked in on the tail end of our conversation.

"Did you take care of our problem?" Jimmy asked.

Carlo took a seat on the couch opposite my father and me. Antonio walked to the bar and poured a glass of scotch. He knocked the drink back and poured another one.

"I did, and have you heard any word from your contacts at Interpol or the FBI on Sabrina?" Antonio asked.

Narrowing my eyes at Jimmy, waiting to hear his response, my phone chimed.

"Sonny's messaging me."

I put him on point with finding any information he could possibly dig up on Sabrina's kidnapping.

"Antonio, focus on what's important. This girl probably just ran off with her friends or something on vacation."

"That's ridiculous. You honestly think she'd take a vacation and be away from me for over a year almost. Yes, we had problems, but Sabrina wouldn't just run off without telling me or her family where she went," Antonio responded, getting frustrated.

I can see the tension on my brother's face and how red he turned at our father thinking she just up and left. Our mom chose that moment to walk into the living room, and we all let a sigh of relief out.

"Boys, are you ready for dinner?" Mom asked.

She stepped toward Antonio and kissed his cheek. Taking him in an embrace and pulling away to look into his eyes, she could see how the stress of not having Sabrina around was affecting him.

"Cara, we'll come in for dinner in a minute. I need to speak with our boys," Dad told her.

"Sure, don't be long though. We have a date tonight."

"Bruno, how is Liz doing?"

All eyes glared at me.

"Liz, the best friend of Sabrina and Janice?" Carlo said.

"Seriously, Bruno, coming from the guy who gave me

shit about dating Sabrina and working with our father to break us up," Antonio stated with a humorless chuckle.

"Maria, please leave us for a minute. It seems our boys are keeping secrets we didn't know about that can affect this family."

"This is bullshit!"

"Antonio. I just got word from our contact in Italy."

I looked down at the message that Sonny just texted me. His contact spotted Sabrina in a motel room. Walking over to him, I saw the photo of Sabrina walking inside the room with a bag of groceries.

"Fuck, did he say if anyone's with her? She's been in Italy for a year, with who?"

"Sonny said Alex was spotted with her a few weeks ago. He said she's been alone for the past two days," I said.

"We don't have time for this. Antonio, you need to move up the shipment deal."

Antonio poured another glass of scotch and placed it down on the table. Sneering at his father, he smirked then headed toward the front door. He stopped with his hand on the doorknob and turned around. Carlo followed him.

"Bruno, send Sonny in to bring her back home, and old man, you'd do well to remember you're speaking with the new Don."

CHAPTER FOUR

JANICE

The constant ringing of my phone pulled me out of my distraction of a dinner with Carlo.

"You need to tell your little boyfriend you're busy for the night."

I looked up at Carlo and smiled, dreading having to tell him the truth about me.

"Hey, hey, what's wrong, baby?"

"I'm fine."

Getting up from my seat, I took our plates to the kitchen. Carlo walked in and wrapped his hands around my waist.

"I'm a good listener."

Kissing my neck and ear, I moaned and stopped preparing the dishes for cleaning to turn around in his arms.

"Mmm… let's take this to the bedroom."

As we walked out of the kitchen, my phone rang again, and Carlo walked over to pick it up.

"Who's Trevor?"

"Nobody. Actually, can we cut this date short? I need to be alone."

Snatching my phone from Carlo's hand, I start to walk back into the kitchen, but Carlo pulled me back into his arms. I struggled to get out of his arms.

"Let me in baby."

Carlo trailed kisses down my back and rubbed a hand under my shirt, twisting my nipple and biting my neck.

"I can't… Carlo"

"Let me in, baby," Carlo moaned into my neck and captured my earlobe with his tongue.

"You don't play fair."

Pulling off my shirt and unbuckling his pants, I dropped down to my knees, pulled his bulge out, and licked the tip down to his balls.

A rush of heat ran over me as I continued to please him.

His right brow shot up in amusement. I glanced up, looking into his eyes, and smiled at what I was about to do.

I slowly rubbed the tip and squeezed, gently putting a little pressure on him. I kissed the tip and rubbed my other hand up his stomach and across his chest.

"Shit, Janice."

"Yes, baby."

Placing his member in my mouth, I put my hands on his hips and slowly took him to the back of my throat, causing his knees to buckle like water. Before I could continue, he pulled me up off the floor and yanked my shorts down roughly.

"You've been a bad girl."

I enjoyed the feeling of his hands roaming up and down my thighs. Hovering with his tall frame over my back with his member sitting at my sex, I could feel the pre-cum leaking out. Turning my head, he pulled my hair and deepened the kiss. Our tongues moved in sync, and his dick slid into my pussy.

"I swear to God you better not ever give my pussy away."

"Who said this was your pussy?"

Slapping my ass and letting my hair go, I fell on the couch as he placed my leg over the armrest.

"Shit, Carlo, I'm not that fucking limber."

"Shut the fuck up," he hissed in my ear.

His strokes were fast and deep. I writhed underneath him.

"Fuck… Tell me you belong to me," Carlo whispered, out of breath.

"Ughh… God, Carlo, wait."

He pulled out of me before I could get my first orgasm. I turned around with an evil scowl on my face.

"What the fuck are you doing? Where are you going?"

Carlo pulled his boxers up and grabbed my phone.

"Do you belong to me? Answer the question, and then I may let you have an orgasm."

Seeing as how I needed to let off some stress, I agreed to his demand and turned my phone completely off.

"Kiss me and meet me upstairs, Daddy. I'll show you how much I belong to you and, for the record, if you ever pull out and not let me get a nut again, you'll catch these hands."

CHAPTER FIVE

SABRINA

*O*ne *week later*

"I know, sweetie. Mommy's going to get us out of here."

"Argggahhh…. agh," AJ cried.

Watching over my shoulder hadn't been easy. Fearing that Alex may have followed my steps was the reason I couldn't use any type of credit card. Even though he took everything from me, I stole his credit card, thinking I could steal some money from it. Patting AJ on the back to get him to calm down was another job in itself. He was hungry, needed changing, and I was on my last euro, paying for this hotel room.

Pulling everything out of my bag, I found all the documents Alex stole, including my passport, ID, and birth certificate.

I stumbled across some jewelry I stole from Alex.

"Selling this would get me a plane ticket out of here."

A knock at the door echoed throughout the room. I froze in place before opening.

"Room service," a male voice said cheerfully.

I stood at the curtain, looking out at the four men standing at my door.

"I didn't order anything."

Another knock at the door.

"We have a delivery for a Sabrina Washington or Bella."

"He found me," I whispered.

Pulling the door open and seeing a group of men all wearing dark-tailored suits and holding guns, stopped me in my track.

"Are you Sabrina Washington or Bella?"

I responded with a nod of my head, saying yes. I finally caught a break from all the torture Alex put me through when running around Italy with minimal resources.

"Who are you and where is Antonio?"

"You'll see him soon. I'm Sonny; I work for Antonio and his family. Pack up your things and grab your son. We have a plane waiting for you."

"What about Alex?"

"That's being handled already. Just grab your son, and we can get you back home to your family."

Agreeing to leave the conversation alone for now, I walked back into the hotel room and grabbed AJ while the rest of the men picked up our things and placed them in the car.

"How did you know I was here?"

"He wouldn't give up on finding you and when Antonio's determined, there's nothing anyone can do to stop him. I'll just say this, with you finally coming home, a lot of deaths will be prevented."

"What do you mean? Antonio killed people?"

"You have no clue who the father of your child is, do you?"

"I'm not naïve. I know he's in deep with the mafia."

"I suggest you have a talk with him and let him explain everything to you."

"Just tell me. After everything I've been through with Alex, I can't take any more surprises, especially with my son involved!"

Sonny narrowed his eyes at me in shock.

"He's the new Don, or how they like to call it in America, the Capo."

I felt lightheaded at the mention of those words. My palms were sweating, my chest aching, and my throat was closing in on me.

"Hold up, the new Don… a Capo?

"Listen, Sabrina, the De Luca Cartel not only runs legitimate businesses, but some illegal ones as well. I've told you too much already. Let Antonio explain it to you when you get home."

"Stop the car?"

"What?"

"I said stop this car, goddammit!"

Sonny gestured with a wave of his hand to the driver to pull over.

"Sabrina, we have instructions to bring you and AJ home. Anything outside of that will need to be dealt with when you see Antonio."

"Let me out of this car. I'm not going back to that lying son of a bitch. It's his fault I'm even in this bullshit."

"Please just calm down."

I yanked the car door open and grabbed AJ's and my bags.

"Tell him to go to hell. This is his entire fault. I should have stayed away when I met him at Ryde the first night and could have avoided dealing with Camilla and Alex's crazy asses."

"Listen, just take the car to the jet, and we'll find

another ride. Please think about your son. This is about getting you back home and reunited with your family. I'll even find another flight for me and my guys, so you'll have the entire plane to yourself."

I took my time contemplating his suggestion and looked down at AJ sleeping in my arms. Hearing that Antonio was the leader of a mafia cartel now was something I never planned on dealing with, let alone raising a child with a Capo. I knew he was in deep, and his father was trying to keep him away from his legit businesses. But knowing they had no regard for human life... Watching and seeing the destruction that the mafia caused over the years, from drug smuggling, murder, and violence in our city had me rethinking the person I'd been sleeping with.

"Fine, I'll take the flight back. But no one inform him about me coming back. Antonio and I are done. Do I make myself clear?"

"Yes."

CHAPTER SIX

CARLO

*L*ying in bed with Janice's beautiful, soft, plump, round ass pressed against me had me wanting to tattoo her name over my heart with a lock and key. She was it for me. We didn't fall asleep until about three a.m. Now I was up at seven, ready for round two.

I ran my hand up and down her smooth chocolate skin.

"Mmmm… yes, baby?" Janice whimpered into my chest.

"Baby, I need you."

Early on in our relationship, I learned Janice liked pleasure and pain. Placing small bites and kisses right after got her juices flowing.

"Baby, you're so wet. Fuck, I need to be inside you," I grumbled.

"Carlo, let me get thirty more minutes of sleep. Then I'll take care of your little friend."

She groggily mumbled and placed her hand on my dick under the covers, then rubbed back and forth. Leaning over, I kissed her neck, down to her shoulder blade, and ear.

"Baby, you can't tease me like this and expect me to leave you alone."

Turning over, Janice slowly opened one eye with a sexy smirk.

"Sweetie, one thing we both know is that I'm not a tease. Since you won't let me sleep, come on. Jump up here and have at it. I'll give you a good hour before I need to get some more sleep before work."

I couldn't stop the glare. We both burst into laughter at her statement.

"Janice, where have you been all my life?"

"Here in Queens. If you don't know, better ask around. Now since you refuse to let me sleep, I'll meet you in the shower so we can finish this little discussion."

She leaned over and kissed my lips, then ran her hand down my chest onto my boxer briefs and pat my little friend who bricked up at her touch.

"Last one in the shower has to do the cooking for a week," I joked and watched as she bolted up out of bed and ran to the bathroom. Shaking my head and laughing, I ran after her and grabbed her from behind.

"Baby, I'll do the cooking and dishes for the rest of our lives if I can have you forever."

Tensing up at my words, she turned around in my arms and wrapped her hands around my neck.

"Are you sure about that?"

Kissing her left, then right cheek, following a trail down her chest, I placed her up against the sink. Burying my head between her legs, I latched onto her clit.

"Jesus… Baby… Shit," she moaned, while holding my head in place with one hand.

"This pussy tastes so good," I murmured as I tortured her with back-to-back orgasms. Seeing her body tremble in my arms, I sucked her clit even faster.

"Yes, Carlo, right there…"
"Give me one more, baby."
"I'm… I'mmm cummm… Oh God!"

CHAPTER SEVEN

LIZ

$\mathcal{W}$alking into Antonio's home, I noticed him sitting on the lounge chair in the same clothes he'd had on for the last two days with boxes lingering on the table, plus half-filled alcohol bottles.

"Have you spoken with her?" Antonio asked.

"I did, and she's adamant about not coming back."

"How's my son?"

"He's big, spoiled, and looks just like you."

"She hates me this time, doesn't she?"

Agreeing with his statement, I cleared my throat to try to soften the blow.

"Antonio, I think she needs time. Finding out you're the head of some drug cartel was pretty huge and overwhelming, especially after she got kidnapped."

"My business ties had nothing to do with her getting kidnapped. It was her ex-stalker fiancé that caused all of this."

I could see the aggression clearly written on his face as if someone took a permanent marker and wrote 'attention, pissed off alpha male alert' right across his forehead. He stood from the chair and slung it across the room.

"Where is she?"

"She doesn't want to see you, Antonio."

"Where is my son?"

Feeling like my life could be in danger if I didn't leave, I stood and grabbed my purse.

"Liz, I suggest you tell me where she is, and I'll avoid having you followed. Remember, I'm the Capo of the cartel now, so my reach is extensive."

"You son of a bitch!"

He gripped my elbow and turned me around. I smacked him across the face and stepped back before he could hit me.

"What the hell is going on in here?" Bruno demanded.

"Thank God you got here before this lunatic kills me."

Antonio rolled his eyes and placed his hands on top of his head in frustration.

"She won't tell me where my son is, and I'm getting tired of the games."

"I understand this is hard on you."

"Hard on me!"

Jumping from his reaction, I moved toward Bruno, ready to leave before he exploded again.

"Liz, judging by your reaction, I can tell you're afraid of Sabrina and me as well. What you should take heed in is the fact that, as the Capo of this family, I will do anything to protect the people I love. My son is my top priority. I suggest you inform your friend that if she doesn't contact me..."

"Are you threatening me?" Liz asked somberly.

"Let yourself out."

CHAPTER EIGHT

DERRICK

As I sat in the undercover van and listened in on Antonio's conversation with Liz, they'd given me a bright idea. I made a small attempt at Sabrina a year ago when I bumped into her at the airport, then again at her office building. Of course, she thought it was it by accident, but we always planned to make contact and bring Antonio and the De Luca Cartel down by any means necessary. I didn't figure it would hurt having a little fun in the process.

"What's the night shift looking like, D?" Jacob, my partner of three years, asked me. We'd been partners ever since we'd been on the force from training, foot patrol, and now DEA.

"Thinking we head back to the precinct and let the second duty take over watching him. You have Connor and Andrew on Sabrina, right?"

"Yeah," he said. "She's at home right now with her son. I still can't believe that beautiful woman has a child by that monster."

"Not for long. She'll have me calling him stepson after

we put Antonio away for life if I have anything to say about it."

Turning the key in the ignition and pulling off from outside of Ryde, we headed back to headquarters.

"What's cooking in that head of yours?"

"You remember when I made contact with her a year ago at the airport, and then we had dinner." He nodded in remembrance as I continued speaking, "I'm going to set up another lunch meeting, possibly dinner, and see about becoming an investor at her company."

Jacob rubbed his chin in thought with a grimace across his face.

"You don't look thrilled with my plan."

Shrugging his shoulders with a nonchalant attitude, I parked the car and walked into the police station.

"Are you doing this to lock Antonio up because he's the head of the cartel or to get close to Sabrina?"

"We both know the cartel is dangerous and, if we can take them down, we'll bring all the families down. Also, we'll get a raise as lieutenants. This benefits us, and if she just happens to be feeling lonely and needs a shoulder to cry on, why should I deny her that shoulder?"

As we walked through the precinct, I found the captain hovering at my desk with an angry scowl on his face.

"My office, now, Derrick!" our captain yelled out as he turned his back toward us.

I turned to Jacob, silently asking if he knew what was up. He shook his head and inaudibly answered no.

"Tell me why I get a call from the mayor, asking me about my two top DEA agents sitting outside Antonio De Luca's place of business."

I was thankful to be standing against the wall. Otherwise, my legs would have given out.

"Captain…"

"Save it. I told you the only way to pull this off was to be legit with all the moves you made. Do you not understand how connected this family is?" He placed both hands on his desk and leaned over, staring into my eyes.

"Captain, everything is going according to plan. You can't pull us out now when I've gotten closer than anyone ever has with this family."

"Son, I understand you're looking to score big with arresting Antonio and his family, but you're doing sloppy work. I hear you've been trying to contact some woman named Sabrina Washington."

"She's Antonio's girlfriend and the mother of his child," Jacob answered.

"Tell me about her and don't leave anything out."

"She's hot." Jacob smirked as the captain and I looked toward him in disbelief with his answer.

"Sabrina's the daughter of Jonathan and Candice Washington, a very well-known family in the city."

"Aren't they the ones who put on that charity function every year and donate to the widow's fund of fallen police officers?"

"Yes, sir."

"And you think she has something to do with Antonio and the cartel business?"

"I think she got caught up with the wrong man and found out who he really is…"

"Wait, are you saying they aren't together at the moment?"

"As far as our surveillance has shown, she was kidnapped and found out it was because of someone trying to get revenge against Antonio. She has since learned he's a leader of a mafia family."

"That's it."

"What's it?"

"The mayor must have spoken with Jonathan about his daughter and…"

"Are you saying Jonathan is into the cartel business?"

"Let me marinate on a few things, and I'll get back to you. I don't think so, but the mayor wouldn't hound me unless it was big. For right now, just stick to as little contact with Antonio as possible. We know he had something to do with Spencer, Camilla, and Alfredo being killed. They've all had contact with Sabrina, and now they end up dead."

"Don't forget Alex has gone missing as well."

"Who's Alex?"

"Sabrina's ex-fiancé. They were all involved with her kidnapping."

"You have proof of this?"

"No, but I'm making progress."

"All right, just keep your heads above water and watch your backs. Our evidence is fragile at the moment without any witnesses. We're only able to prove Antonio had a hand in giving the word to end them. The evidence is only linked to some of his low-level killers. No one is rolling on him. They'll go to jail for life first, before snitching."

As Jacob and I walked out of the captain's office, I saw a familiar face stepping into the interrogation room. I tapped Jacob on the shoulder and motioned at what had my attention.

"Maybe our luck is finally changing for the better."

Smirking at his response, we both sat at our desks and watched as a police officer talked with Adriana Ricci, the Donna of the Ricci Family and Camilla's mother.

CHAPTER NINE

SABRINA

Watching AJ play around in the bathtub with the bubbles and giggling made all the heartache worthwhile. Becoming a mother and protector of my son was my priority. At some point, I needed to let Antonio see his son. I couldn't keep him or his lifestyle away from AJ. Something had to give because I couldn't continue down this path of destruction.

"I hope he doesn't think you'll be in that, AJ."

I loved kissing his little nose as he giggled. I picked him up out of the tub and placed a towel around him, kissing both cheeks as he squirmed in my arms. I drained the water from the tub as I froze at the words he'd spoken.

"I would never do anything to harm my son. Baby, I made a mistake," Antonio told me, coming from nowhere.

"What are you doing here?" I sucked my teeth and rolled my eyes, as I pushed my way out of the bathroom. I walked over to check my phone and saw a message from Liz, letting me know she'd spoken with Antonio and gave him my address.

"Liz told me where you were."

He walked closer to me and took AJ out of my hands.

"Hey, little man. I'm your daddy."

"Did you hurt her?"

He froze at the words I just spoke. Placing a kiss on AJ's forehead, Antonio laid him down on the bed before wrapping the comforter over him.

"What did you just say?"

I opened my mouth to speak, and nothing came out. I got some encouragement after all the months I'd been away from my family and having AJ by myself. I blacked out and smacked him in the face.

"Get out!"

"Bella, I know you've been through a lot, so I'll let you take your anger out on me this one time. After we talk and I explain everything, you and our son are coming home with me."

Cocking my head to the side and balling up my fist, I was ready to punch him in the face. He looked down at my hand and shook his head in frustration.

"Baby, you need to calm down."

"I need to calm down. What I need is for you to leave me the hell alone. Going forward, my lawyer will have a schedule for visitation with AJ, and as far as us, this is over, playboy. I'm done."

As I went to open my apartment door, Antonio grabbed my arm, pulled me back into his chest, and placed his hand right hand around my throat, lightly squeezing and moving his left hand under my skirt. I smacked his hand away, and he bit my ear and kissed the pain away.

"Stop. Baby, you and I both know this will never be over."

Moving his index finger toward my panties, he ripped them off.

"I was wrong for not telling you. I apologize for everything that's happened."

"I don't need your apology. What we need is to leave each other alone and co-parent AJ. This is just too much for me. I was fucking kidnapped by some crazy bitch."

"Fine."

"What…"

Pulling his hand out of my panties and releasing my throat, I felt hurt by his sudden rejection. Once again, he wasn't fighting for us, or maybe I was the one not fighting.

"I'll leave you alone and give you space. That's what you want, right?"

"Ummm… Yeah."

"Can I see AJ before I go?"

"Yes and—"

"Don't worry, I won't be long."

Before I could stop him, my phone lit up with Liz's name. That reminded me, I needed to set up a lunch or something to let everyone know that I was back.

"Hello."

"Hey, Are you all right?"

Clearing my throat, I tried my best to hold back the tears.

"I'm fine, Liz. What's going on with you?"

"Sabrina, we've known each other for how many years now? So please spare me the fake 'I'm fine' and talk to me."

"I just… I."

Watching Antonio walk back into the living room, I wiped the tears before they fell. We both stared into each other's eyes, and he started to say something.

"Hello, Sabrina… Hello?"

"Sorry, Liz, what did you say?"

As I turned my back to the door and took my shoes off, Antonio walked out without saying goodbye.

"You sound like you need an intervention or tequila. Let me call Janice."

"Please don't call that crazy girl. I'll be fine."

"You don't sound like it, Sabrina. I understand you can't talk about everything that happened to you over there with your family or me. But you need to talk with someone."

"As soon as I get AJ adjusted to things and schedule visitation with Antonio."

"Schedule visitation for what? Is Antonio causing problems?" Janice asked.

Janice walked in without knocking.

"I gave you that key for emergencies. Not to just pop in whenever you feel like it."

She waved me off, walked into the kitchen, and came back with a bottle of wine.

"Who's on the phone?"

Taking her shoes and jacket off, I noticed she had a hickey on her neck.

"I see someone's been living it up with a new man."

"You could too if you let him. Again, I ask what is this scheduled-visitation stuff?"

"Liz, let me call you tomorrow. We'll have lunch or something."

"Hey, boo, she probably will stand you up as she did me the other day. So plan on a backup date."

Waving her off, I heard Liz laughing in the background before I hung up.

"Girl, you know I already figured she'd bail on me. I have my man on standby if that happens."

"Did she just say my man on standby?" I muttered to myself.

"See what happens when you hibernate away from people."

"I think trying to cope with adjusting back to my

surroundings is a legitimate reason for shutting myself away in my apartment."

"Sabrina, you can tell everyone else anything, and they'll believe it. But as your best friend, I know the real you. So, this façade you're putting on stops now."

Getting up to check on AJ, I grabbed my phone to see if Antonio had called or left a message. Walking into the nursery, I noticed his blanket pulled up, and a small stuffed teddy bear was placed next to him.

"You can't run away from him."

"Shit. Janice, you scared me."

"Good, now let my godson sleep in peace, and you help me finish off this bottle of wine."

Walking back into the living room, I grabbed the glass off the table and watched her pour the wine.

"How are you feeling?"

"Frustrated and pissed off. This whole thing is just insane. I don't know what to do about Antonio."

"Do you love him?"

Taking a sip of wine, I placed it down on the table.

"What does that have to do with anything?"

"A lot. Yes, he lied about who he is, but deep down, you knew he wasn't a boy scout."

"Janice, you don't understand. I have a child with this man. We're connected for the rest of our lives. Yes, I knew he wasn't some squeaky-clean guy. We're talking about a mafia boss. I just need to think about my future and AJ's.

"Well, keep thinking because no matter what you come up with, you're still going to belong to him, just like I belong to Carlo. The second Antonio laid eyes on you at Ryde, you became the Donna of the De Luca Cartel."

"Don't remind me. Are you spending the night?" I asked.

"Hell no. I need dick next to me when I sleep," Janice informed her.

"You seriously need a reality check. I have to take AJ to my mom's in the morning. I'll talk to you later."

"Good night, and stop being stubborn!" Janice shouted as she walked toward the front door, letting herself out.

Gesturing with a shrug of my shoulders, I walked off toward my bedroom, contemplating seeing my parents tomorrow.

* * *

WAKING up nine hours later after tossing and turning, I woke up still feeling betrayed and hurt from Antonio's lies. Hearing my phone ring and AJ crying, I picked it up to answer my mom's call.

"Morning, Mom," I answered groggily.

"I'm so glad you're back safe and sound. Come open the door. My hands are full," Candice asked cheerfully.

"Wait, you're outside right now?" I questioned, jumping out of bed fast, looking around for my robe.

"We are, and you need to hurry up before our arms fall off."

"We who?"

"Sabrina, I am your mother; don't question me. Just come open the door, girl."

Tripping over a pair of shoes, I silently cursed to myself to avoid waking AJ since he finally quieted down. Taking my scarf off my head and tightening my robe, I reached the door and opened it, surprised to see my sister Ashley with my mom.

"What are you doing here, Ashley? I thought you had a big surgery today."

Ashley followed my mom, walking past me toward the kitchen with bags of food.

"We couldn't wait to see my precious grandbaby," Candice replied while pulling food containers out and grabbing plates out of the cabinet.

"I have that later today. Mom told me last night about you coming over, and we just decided to surprise you with food this morning," Ashley answered while placing an arm around my shoulders and hugging me tight.

"Thanks for the food. Where's Dad?

"At the office. He said for you to come in today and bring AJ so everyone can see him. Matter of fact, why am I the last one to know about you and Antonio breaking up?"

Taking a bite of the pancakes and avoiding her disappointed look into my eyes, I turned toward Ashley to try to make small talk.

"How's the life of a surgeon?" I asked.

"Oh honey, you can't avoid the question forever," Mom replied.

"I thought you and Dad would be happy. Most parents would like for their daughter to avoid the bad boys."

"That's true. Unfortunately, you've never been the type of daughter to listen to what your father and I have to say."

"She's right about that, sis."

Taking a fork and stealing a sausage off Ashley's plate, I stuck my tongue out at her in defiance.

"Heyyyy..."

"Don't get mad at your sister because she's telling the truth. Anyway, I want to see my grandbaby. Go get cleaned up, and I'll watch him for you."

Eating the last piece of sausage off Ashley's plate, I placed a kiss on my mom's cheek and walked to the bedroom to get dressed for the day.

"Follow me and, Ashley, can you grab the bottle out of

the fridge and warm it up? He usually wakes up around this time."

"Wow, my baby has a baby."

"Yep. Candice Washington is a grandma."

"Girl, bye, ain't no grandma over here. I'm too fly for that."

"First off, saying too fly makes you old. So, I suggest you think of some other type of slang to use."

Opening the door to AJ's room, we slowly walked in, admiring him as he slept under his blanket.

"He's so beautiful. I can't believe you have a baby."

Ashley passed the bottle over to my mom. AJ sneezed in his sleep, and I wiped his noise.

"Sabrina, let us take him for the day. You have work and Antonio to deal with. Besides, you need a shower and, from the looks of it, some sleep."

"Are you sure?"

"Positive. Besides, you need a little time on your own. I know you've been through a lot this past year. I spoke with Antonio and before you yell at me, I'm a grown woman, and you're my child. I have every right to speak with my son-in-law."

"Excuse me, we're not together."

"That's what your mouth says. Now get dressed and leave us alone," Mom demanded.

Shaking my head in annoyance, I left AJ's room, agreeing to let my mom and sister babysit for the day. Heading into my room, I walked into my closet to find something to wear for the day, since Liz invited me to lunch with her and Janice.

CHAPTER TEN

LIZ

I knew many people would be surprised at me, myself included. One thing I'd always prided myself on was honesty and living in my truth. Lately, that hadn't been happening with my friends. I'd kept a secret from them, and I needed to tell them before they found out another way. To see the disappointment on Janice and Sabrina's faces would just kill me, which was why I was having this meeting before they came to make sure we were both serious about what was happening.

"Baby… stop worrying." Bruno caressed my cheek softly, and I leaned into his palm.

"I just want to make sure we're in this together and not making a mistake."

"You think we're a mistake?" Bruno pulled his hand back, and his body tensed.

"No."

"Then tell me what has you so scared to tell people about us. Are you ashamed of me?" The hurt in his voice made me even more scared to tell him the truth.

"Of course not, Bruno. Honestly, we both come from different worlds, and your family is very—"

Seeing the frown on his face, I took a sip of water before continuing.

"I see what Sabrina and Antonio go through, and I don't want that for us. Just let me do the talking when they get here, okay?"

"I'm done being a secret, Elizabeth. Either you're with me or not."

"Bruno."

He motioned for me to look over my shoulder as Sabrina and Janice walked through the door. Taking another sip of my water, I waited for them to approach the table.

"Heyyyy… Liz… um… Bruno, what are you doing here?" Sabrina asked as she sat next to me at the table as Janice sat next to Bruno.

"I'll let Liz answer that."

"Is this an intervention for Sabrina and Antonio? You know I'm the real Iyanla: Fix my Life. She stole that show from me," Janice joked as she talked with the waitress about ordering a glass of wine.

"What!" Sabrina screeched and jumped from her seat.

"Girl, sit down. You know everybody's over your drama with Antonio."

"Janice, shut up. Sabrina, please sit down. I called this lunch meeting for myself." All eyes turned toward me. I reached across the table and grabbed Bruno's hand. Seeing a surprised look on Janice and Sabrina's faces, I continued speaking. "Bruno and I are dating. Before you say anything, let me finish. It started after you went missing, Sabrina. Janice and I did everything we could to find you. At the same time, I was dealing with a breakup and a miscarriage."

"Why didn't you tell us?" Sabrina questioned sincerely.

I wiped a tear from my eyes with my napkin. Bruno tightened his grip on my hand.

"So much was going on with you, and then Janice had a lot going on with Carlo. I didn't want to burden anyone with my problems."

"What problems, Liz?" Janice asked.

I hesitated to tell my two best friends about the abuse in my last relationship.

"I didn't just break up with Jeremy because he cheated on me. He hit me, and the stress of the abuse caused me to lose my child," I told them in a rush before I started crying again.

"Where the hell does he live? He had the nerve to put his hands on you. Ohh, just wait till he meets Betsy."

"Janice, calm down," Sabrina demanded as she placed her arm around my shoulders and gave me a tight hug.

"Who's Betsy?" Bruno asked curiously.

"Her gun," we answered in unison.

"I appreciate you both. Bruno helped me out a lot, which is how we've become more than friends."

"Are you happy?"

"Yes... I know the Bruno you see in the streets is some mafia guy. When he's with me, he's sweet, caring, and supportive."

"All I want to know is if the dick is good," Janice joked as our food was placed in front of us.

Bruno smirked and winked as he picked up his fork. Tossing my napkin at Janice, I looked over at Sabrina as she stared off into space.

"Hey, are you all right?"

She smiled and squeezed my hand in comfort.

"I'm fine. Just have a lot on my plate."

"You don't always have to fight your demons alone."

"I know."

We both turned toward Janice and Bruno, who were laughing and joking around.

CHAPTER ELEVEN

SABRINA

After lunch with the girls and Bruno, I decided to bring AJ over to meet his other grandparents. Maria's been calling me all week. I couldn't avoid her anymore. Assuring me that Antonio wouldn't be here, I decided to put my big girl panties on and get this over with. Stepping out and walking around to the passenger door, I unbuckled AJ as he squirmed in my arms and grabbed his baby bag.

"Hey, little man. You ready to meet your grandparents?" As I closed the door and put the baby bag around my shoulders, I planted kisses on each of his tiny little fingers and toes. He giggled and twisted in my arms, teasing him more and placing air bubbles against his jaw. He lightly farted in my arms. I shook my head and laughed at his facial expression.

Approaching the door after security let me pass right through, I rang the doorbell and shifted AJ from my left to right side. After five minutes of waiting, I finally heard the locks turning, Maria opened the door with a surprised smile on her face.

"Sabrina, look at you. Oh my God, it's been so long." Maria pulled me into her arms excitedly. She motioned for me to come inside as the housekeeper walked over to us.

"Sabrina, would you like some iced tea? I was just getting ready to sit down to lunch. Angela can take the baby bag and put his things away."

"Sure… Is Antonio here?"

"No, he's at the club. I did tell him you were coming over though. I hope that was okay."

"That's fine. What about your husband?"

Passing AJ to her, we both walked into the living room to sit down.

"Jimmy's working in his office right now. Listen, Sabrina, I understand my husband can be a little overzealous—"

"Umm… Mrs. De Luca, your husband hates me and thinks that the mixing of our kind is killing his family."

Seeing the distressed concern drift across her face, I watched as she wavered in thought about my last words.

"Jimmy is from the old school. I can agree with you on that, but please don't punish us by not letting AJ be a part of our lives. I'm not sure what's going on with you and Antonio. One minute, you're together, and the next, you're apart. Honestly, it's like a soap opera at this point."

Nodding in agreement, I helped to take AJ's coat and hat off his head.

"Have you talked with Antonio about what happened?"

"Why do you stay with him? I mean in a mafia family… aren't you afraid for your kids?"

"Sabrina, you're a smart girl. You had to have known deep down that Antonio was into some illegal things. Would I have chosen a different route for my boys? Of course, but when you're in love with someone, you compromise."

I realized she was encouraging me to give Antonio another chance with the gleam in her eyes as she spoke about compromise and love.

"Lunch is ready, Mrs. De Luca," Angela said from the front entrance of the living room.

Maria grabbed AJ and pretended to blow bubbles into his stomach as he giggled and clapped his hands.

"I can't believe you had him all by yourself."

"He allowed Valentina and one doctor in the room. I wasn't allowed to leave unless he accompanied me or bodyguards."

"Ohh, sweet Sabrina…"

Afraid to tear up, I gestured for her to go in front of me toward the dining room. We held hands as we walked together.

"Maria, did you find my grey tie?" Jimmy asked as he walked into the dining room.

Ignoring his harsh glare, I took AJ out of Maria's hands and prepared to leave.

"Sabrina, wait—"

"I'm sorry, Maria, but clearly nothing's changed in this family."

"Please wait. You promised I could have some time with my grandson. Jimmy, please leave."

"This is my house. Why do I have to leave?" Jimmy questioned, waving his hands frantically around the room.

"Stop it! I've let you run things with the boys and stayed out of your business with the cartel, but this, you will have nothing to say. I want to have my grandson in my life and if you can't understand that, then I suggest you leave, James."

Standing back with my mouth gaped wide open in shock, I watched a stare down between Antonio's parents.

"Cara, please."

Placing her hands across her chest with her lips poked out, she reminded me of my fights with Antonio. Eventually, one of us gave in to the other.

"Sabrina, have a seat. Jimmy is leaving. Aren't you, dear?"

Seeing big bad Jimmy De Luca cave into his wife's demands was a sight no one would ever believe. Maria grabbed AJ out of my arms again and took a seat back down in her chair. I sat back down as Angela brought our plates out, and we ate and talked.

CHAPTER TWELVE

ANTONIO

Going through some last-minute paperwork at Ryde, I glanced over at the security monitors. A commotion was happening down on the main floor, and I noticed Carlo and Bruno pulling two women away and walking toward the back entrance. I shut the monitor off and continued working when someone knocked on my door.

"Come in."

"We have a problem, Antonio," Bruno stated, shutting the door and taking a seat.

I placed my phone down and focused my attention on Bruno as Carlo stepped into the room.

"What's the problem?" I asked.

Carlo looked from Bruno and back to me, so I nodded for him to continue talking.

"They know about your little send off for Camilla."

Frustrated from the separation with Sabrina and now the Ricci Family poking their noses in their daughter's death, I couldn't catch a break.

"What exactly have you heard?"

"Tony, we have to send a word out to the families that Camilla ran away or something. We can't have a murder hanging over our heads. There's too much going on with the aftermath of Alfredo and the new shipment coming in through the docks. We need to lay low."

Blowing out a breath of frustration, I stood to grab a drink from my bar.

"How did they find out?"

"I think she had a backup plan in case we caught on to her scheme of marrying you."

Bruno took the glass of whiskey out of my hands and drank it before pouring another one.

"We have another problem on our hands, with the DEA breathing down our necks," Bruno said.

"That bitch is still ruining my life, even in the aftermath of her death."

Remembering the night we found out Camilla, Alfredo, and Alex conspired to keep Sabrina and me apart, I grew annoyed all over again and wanted to bring them back from the dead just to torture them again.

"Fuck!"

"Stay focused, little brother. You did what we all would have done to her."

I flashed back to finding a package on my porch. I had thoughts in my mind to kill them right where she stood, but I decided another way for her to be sent to hell permanently.

* * *

FOUR HOURS LATER, she was bent over with her ass in the air, sweat pouring from her skin, hair matted as I pulled it tightly, moving in and out of her with fast, deep, pene-trating strokes.

"Baby... slow downnnn..."

Wrapping my fingers around her throat, I tightened and cut off her circulation a little bit to make her think she was safe before smacking her across the ass.

"Let me hear you scream, baby."

Picking up my pace, she fell flat on the bed as I hovered over her, backsliding in and out of her wet pussy.

"I love you. Ughh, Goddd... When are we getting married?"

Shaking off the thoughts of Sabrina, I distracted Camilla with a kiss to her ear, then shoulders as I wrapped a scarf around my hands.

"Soon as you plan the details, Cara."

"Right there... See, Tony, I told you I was made for you."

Wrapping the scarf around her neck swiftly, she jerked in surprise and tried to fight me off. She breathed hard, scratching at my neck.

"No. No. Camilla, save your breath. I don't want you to die until you explain some things," I whispered.

"Please. Please, Antonio."

Turning her around, I took the scarf away and placed my hand on her throat. Tears built in her eyes. A few years ago, I would have never thought I'd be ready to kill Camilla.

"Confess everything that you're doing with Alfredo, or I'll kill your entire family and make you watch."

"Antonio, please. I'm on your side. Someone has lied to you. That bitch."

"Bitch, pick a side before I pick one for you."

"Okay... I... I was working with Alfredo to break up you and Sabrina. He wanted to take over the cartel, and I wanted to get revenge for my family..." Camilla stuttered out.

Tightening the scarf around her neck, her eyes rolled into the back of her head as her arms loosened around my hands.

"Antonio, Antonio!" Carlo yelled out my name as I thought back on the night I killed Camilla.

"Ughhh, yeah… put in some calls at the mayor's office. We need to know who's watching us and put a stop to it before everything falls down around us like a house of cards."

CHAPTER THIRTEEN

SABRINA

oticing that my family didn't change anything made it more real. I was taken and held hostage as leverage over Antonio.

Placing my purse down and hanging my jacket up, I ran my fingers across my desk and pressed my hand against the pictures lining the wall. My entire world had changed in the blink of an eye.

"Sabrina, I'm so happy you're back," Lisa said

"Lisa, thanks so much for holding down the fort. I truly owe you. Anytime you're ready for a vacation just let me know."

"Well, I may be cashing in on that in a few weeks actually."

Waving her hand in front of my face, I saw a two-carat, heart-shaped diamond engagement ring with small diamonds around the side. Grabbing her hand in excitement, I noticed my father standing at the door.

"Hi, Dad. Did you know about Lisa's engagement?"

He walked into the room and closed the door. Our smiles faded in response to his scowl.

"What's wrong? Did something happen to Mom?"

"Sabrina, have a seat," Dad told me with a somber look in his eyes.

"I'm fine standing. Tell me, is it Ashley?"

He unbuttoned his jacket, grabbed my hand, and we walked over to have a seat on the couch.

"Please tell me Ashley and Mom are okay?"

The tears already started falling.

"Honey, your mom and sister are fine. I can't believe I'm saying this, but the police called me this morning to inform me that Spencer was found dead in his apartment."

"Wait…Wait. I'm going to be sick. This can't be real. He wouldn't, would he?"

"Who wouldn't do what?" Dad questioned with a confused look on his face.

"Huh?"

"I asked you who wouldn't."

"Ugh, nothing… I need some air."

"I know Spencer was a friend of yours, and you may have had something going on at one point."

"Dad, please, I need to take care of something."

"Fine, just call your mother when you get a chance. She wants to see her grandchild again, and Ashley wants you to call her," Dad stated.

"I will later today. I know she's excited about being a grandmother. I just need to take care of a few things, and I'll be back tomorrow to look into Spencer's workload."

My father hugged me tight and placed a kiss on my forehead. Smiling back, I glanced around my office. Nothing had changed.

I'd missed so much over the last year and knowing Spencer was gone because of my relationship with Antonio bothered me.

I grabbed my purse and keys off the desk, and then walked around to kiss my father goodbye and run out of the office.

CHAPTER FOURTEEN

ANTONIO

*H*aving my son in my home, seeing the look in Mom's eyes at her first grandchild, made me want to have more kids with Sabrina. I still couldn't believe she was missing for almost a year and had my first child without me there.

"Antonio, he's so precious," Mom said excitedly.

Glancing at AJ and seeing the smile on his face made this all worth it. I'd do anything for my son, even if that meant leaving Sabrina alone for good.

"Mom, you'll spoil him if you keep picking him up."

"Hush, this is my first bambino. I'll spoil him as much as I want. How are things with Sabrina? Has she come around to the idea of you being a Capo?"

I took a sip of my scotch before, shaking my head, then pinched my nose in irritation at her question. I start to speak before I heard someone banging on the front door.

"Speak of the devil."

Opening the front door, Sabrina had her hands on her hips with a scowl on her face, eyes narrowed, and lips poked out in a pout. If I weren't so pissed off at her for keeping us apart, I'd be turned on at how beautiful she looked. I'd tell my mom to keep AJ and take her right here on the floor.

Sabrina smacked me and walked in without saying a word.

"How could you kill him, Tony?"

"Excuse me."

Pulling her into my chest, she squirmed in my arms.

"What is going on out here?" Maria asked.

"Mrs. De Luca, I didn't know you'd be here."

"Obviously, you didn't judging by the flushed handprint on my son's face."

Letting Sabrina go, I yanked her toward the kitchen, away from my mom and son.

"Care to tell me why you came over here all fired up."

"Where's my son?"

Feeling ballistic and bold, I walked up to Sabrina, placed my hand around her neck, and moved her toward the wall, out of earshot of my mom.

"I've been patient and supportive because of what you've been through over the last year, and even though you continue to place the blame on my shoulders, I'll take it because I love…"

Shaking her head in defense, she tried to get out of my grip. I lifted her by her legs, and she wrapped them around me. Placing a kiss on her lips and easing my tongue inside, we both fought for control.

"I hate you," Sabrina groaned.

"I love you."

Heading toward my guest bedroom down the hall, I walked to the side and locked the door before placing her in the middle of the bed, my lips never leaving hers.

"Why did you kill Spencer?"

Sabrina eased out of my grip and stared into my eyes.

"Because he was a threat to you and me."

Not believing me, Sabrina pushed me off her and jumped up, getting ready to leave the room.

"You can't keep running when things don't go your way, princess."

Turning around and peering up into my face, Sabrina crossed her arms under her breasts and glared into my eyes.

"Say that again, playboy. I keep running, you say."

Finally feeling like I had her attention, I walked over to the bed and lay back down with my hands behind my back and kicked off my shoes.

"If you want answers, I've got the time. Today, we'll solve our problems, and you can't run. If you want to know the real me, then you'll stay in this room."

Rolling her eyes at my suggestion and looking around the room, she checked her watch before she kicked her shoes off. She tried sitting at the edge of the bed, but I pulled her up to sit on my lap.

"I meant what I said, Bella."

"I know, and that's the problem, Antonio. You scare me."

Rubbing up her arms and thighs, I placed a gentle kiss on her forehead.

"Bella, I'll always protect you and, before you start with Camilla and Spencer, let me explain."

"Fine, explain."

"I didn't know anything about Camilla and my uncle plotting against me until it was too late. Spencer was just in the way of me and you."

She slapped me across the chest.

"Ouch, what was that for?"

"Boy, you can't go around killing people because they get in your way."

"Baby, I'm Capo; anything I want I get. Spencer was a means to an end. He wouldn't have stopped coming for you. Then I found out he was stealing from you and me."

"What are you talking about?"

"I'll talk about that another time. Let's discuss us and how you're moving in and having more of my babies."

Blowing out a breath in frustration, Sabrina tried to get out of my grasp, but I tightened my hold.

"Antonio, our issues can't be solved with me having your kids and us living together. I'm hurt that you've hidden who you are from me for months and not to mention, damn near got me killed."

"Bella, I was going to tell you once we got back to my place that night. Things got out of hand, then you were kidnapped, and I was still dealing with the aftermath of my shooting."

"I need time, Antonio."

"You'll have time, just under my roof, end of discussion. Everyone knows you are my future Donna and the mother of my child. I need you protected at all times."

"Sir, I think you have me mistaken with Camilla, boo. I'm not living my life under the thumb of a team of bodyguards."

Hearing my mom and AJ giggling in the living room, I refused to fight with her at this moment. What she didn't know was that all her things were getting packed and moved tonight, with or without her consent.

"How about we take this one step at a time and spend some time with our son?"

"I mean it, Antonio. I'm not moving in until we've had more time to figure out our situation."

Kissing her lips and squeezing her ass, I moaned and pulled her dress down.

"Ahhhh, I thought you wanted to hang with our son?"

"After we've had our little playdate reunion."

Pinching her nipples and squeezing her breasts, I leaned up to suck each breast into my mouth.

"Damniitt… you don't play fair."

"Baby, I'm the Capo. It's in my DNA to get whatever I want, by any means necessary."

Pulling my pants down a little and placing my dick at her opening, Sabrina slid down and closed her eyes in delight.

"Baby, you feel so good and tight."

Sitting in a squatting position, she slowly rode me and tightened her pussy muscles on my dick.

Brushing my fingers against her clit, she cried out in pleasure. The base of my spine tingled as I picked up my pace.

"Antonio… I love!" Sabrina answered breathlessly.

Knocking on my door stopped her movements.

"What are you doing? Keep going."

"It could be important."

"It's not, I promise."

"Antonio, your brother and Carlo are here," Mom said through the door.

"See, now let me down," Sabrina demanded.

"Fuck that, baby. They can wait; I need you."

Before she could protest, I turned us both over with me on top. I grabbed her left leg and placed it over my shoulder, slowly easing my length back into her as she massaged her breasts. I deepened the kiss as I began slow, shallow strokes.

The banging grew louder before Sabrina screamed out.

"Ohh, baby!"

"I'll never let you go, Bella."

CHAPTER FIFTEEN

SABRINA

ntonio and I semi-agreed to work on our relationship, and he would give me space to work things out. At the same time, AJ and I lived under his roof. Well, I protested to have my own room. I wasn't ready to sleep in the same bed as him.

Turning off his car, we looked at each other in amusement at the fight we had earlier today after I discovered he'd moved all my things out of my apartment.

"I still can't believe you did that."

"Bella, you underestimated me. I meant it when I said I wouldn't let anything stand in our way, even you. We belong together, and no one can do anything about it."

"Yes, sir."

"You know what that does to me when you call me sir."

"I do, and you know we can't do anything because we're meeting my family, and I need you on your best behavior."

"Of course, baby. Does your family know about me, specifically my family?"

As we walked, he rubbed my ass. I stopped at the mention of his family's business. Turning and looking into his eyes, I smiled and thought of an excuse to give my family.

"I only told them about your club business. Depending on how far things go with us, then we can discuss your family and my family meeting."

A smirk crossed Antonio's face, and I saw the wheels already turning in his head.

"I see I'm not the only one in this relationship who hides secrets."

My sister opened the door as we knocked.

"Sabrina, you finally came," Ashley said excitedly as she hugged me and shook Antonio's hand.

"Hey, Ashley. This is Antonio."

"Nice to meet you, Ashley. I'm her fiancé, Antonio."

I staggered at his words, and Ashley smiled at me.

"I like him."

"Ashley, please doesn't encourage his behavior. We're not engaged; he's just my baby daddy."

Wrapping his arms around my shoulders, Antonio kissed my left cheek and pinched my ass.

"Ouch, that hurt."

"Look who the cat dragged in, my baby girl," Dad said.

I embraced my dad and kissed him on the cheek, noticing Antonio stand back and hold a hard glare on his face.

"Antonio, I would say it's good to see you again. I don't think we need to fake it for anyone."

"I'm here for Sabrina."

"What's going on, Dad?"

Ashley and I looked at each other, then at our father and Antonio in disbelief. These two knew each other.

"Dinner is ready," Mom informed us as we followed her and my father to the dining room. Antonio gripped my hand and tightened his hold.

"I'm not running, baby."

Hoping to reassure her, he loosened his hold, and we sat for dinner.

"So, Antonio, I hear you're the successful owner of the Ryde nightclub. That's where you met Sabrina, correct?"

I wiped both sides of my mouth and took a sip of water as Antonio answered, "That's correct, Mrs. Washington. I saw her, and at first sight, I just knew she'd be mine. Now we have a son together, and hopefully, she'll agree to be my wife in the future."

Complete silence engulfed the room, and my dad's expression darkened.

"Marriage, really, Sabrina?" Mom asked curiously.

Not wanting to rock the boat, I stayed silent.

"She's shy at the moment. But we both are excited about bringing another baby into the fold."

"Sabrina, are you crazy?! He's a killer for God's sake," Dad shouted and jumped out of his seat.

We all watched him pace back and forth.

"Mr. Washington. I'm no killer, unless provoked."

All eyes went to Antonio, and I could have just fallen into a hole and never came out. Leaving my parents' house before dessert was even served was for the best. I knew we couldn't work in a real relationship with his temper. No matter the situation, it would always come back to killing. I ignored him on the ride back home, stared out of the window.

* * *

SLAMMING my purse down on the kitchen counter, I grabbed a bottled water and walked out of the kitchen toward my room.

"Sabrina, don't walk away from me," Antonio demanded.

"I can't believe the way you acted with my parents. This is the exact reason why we won't work."

His face reddened, and his mouth snapped shut. Seeing him speechless had me regretting my words.

"Antonio, wait. I didn't—"

Waving me off, he walked toward his bedroom upstairs.

"At what point do I come first?"

Feeling a gut punch to my stomach, I let him walk out of the room and thought over the question, seriously contemplating my answer.

CHAPTER SIXTEEN

DERRICK

I sat listening to Jacob and the backup squad give me the rundown on the latest shipyard deal Antonio was setting up. I planned on hitting him another way as Jacob and the team scoped out the warehouse.

"D, have you made contact with her?" Jacob inquired as he passed me a wire to hide in my cufflinks.

"I'm meeting her for a lunch date."

"You told the captain it was a work meeting.

"That's what I said."

"Are you catching feelings for her? Because if you are, then we need to pull you off this case."

I waved him off at his suggestion of me falling in love. Only one woman had my heart, and she was no longer with me.

"Just focus on the mission. We need you to get close to her and find out as much as possible about this upcoming deal."

"Didn't the guys say she hasn't spoken to him in a few days? I think they broke up."

"D, seems like you're making excuses to not press her. I

find that odd since you were the one who wanted to bring her in on this sting."

"Jacob, don't insult me. I started this case and brought you in. Sabrina Washington is a pawn—nothing more, nothing less."

Throwing his hands up in surrender, we tapped hands and let the petty argument go.

"Where are you meeting her for lunch?"

"A spot around the corner from her office, Gold Post or something?"

"Do you have surveillance inside and outside?"

Shaking my head, I grabbed my watch and shades off the table.

"I'm not expecting anything besides us going through paperwork on a few deals."

"I recommend placing at least someone on the inside."

Waving off the suggestion, I picked up my phone and called Sabrina to confirm, placing my finger against my lips for everyone in the room to be quiet.

"Hello," Sabrina answered cheerfully.

"Hey, Miss Washington, are we still on for our lunch date?"

"Derrick, must I always remind you to call me Sabrina? Yes, we're still meeting for lunch. Did you have any ideas on companies that you need me to bring research about? I have a personal list."

"Just bring your beautiful self. The rest we'll work out later."

Hearing a long sigh on the other end, I chastised myself for letting my flirtation get out of hand.

"Derrick, you do understand I'm just working with you on a business level. I'm already in a sticky situation with my boyfriend."

"I understand, Sabrina, but last time we talked, you didn't have a boyfriend. Are you back together with him?"

"Enough about my personal life. We have money to make, and I can't do that while on the phone. See you for lunch, Derrick."

"See you soon, Sabrina."

Hanging up the phone, I lifted my gaze and saw Jacob looking at me.

CHAPTER SEVENTEEN

ANTONIO

Meeting with the cartel was the perfect distraction from the latest fallout with Sabrina and her insecurities. After taking care of Alfredo, Camilla, and Alex, we had a new shipment coming in that required my attention, since it was coming in through a shipyard.

"Antonio, we've trained and gone over the layout multiple times. I still think we need extra guards on the corner levels and front bank," Sonny stated.

"How many loads are we expecting?" Carlo asked.

"I need our best guys on this, no fuck ups like last time. I'm still looking into how we got hit by the Russians."

Everyone nodded in agreement.

"Expecting about twenty cases of ammo and paintings blocked out," Bruno answered.

"How's the little bambino, Antonio?"

Hearing my father ask about his grandson caught me off guard. Since they'd been back in my life, we stayed clear of each other. Mom was the one who spent the most time with him. Even Bruno had seen him and hung out.

"He's doing great. You should come over to see him some time."

His blue eyes lit up at me, asking him to hang out with his grandson.

"I'd like that. Your mother is always on the phone with Sabrina doing that FaceTime junk and laughing at everything he does. If I didn't know any better, I'd think she wanted another baby."

"Pops, that's the last thing I ever want to hear about from you and mom, having another baby at your age."

"He's right, Dad. Some things you need to leave be. We have our son now, and he's getting all the attention from the ladies."

"Since we're all set for the shipyard, what's happening with the Ricci family and Camilla's burial?"

All eyes looked at each other and avoided my question.

"I take it from the silence in this room that we have a little situation on our hands."

"Son, I didn't want to bring this up. But after you had Spencer and Camilla killed, we've seen an increase in individuals asking questions."

"Who?"

"My contact at the station said there's a guy out there named Derrick Smith looking into you."

I clenched my jaw in aggravation. That son of a bitch who went on a date with Sabrina was an undercover agent. Slamming my hand down on the table, the entire room jumped in surprise.

Pulling my phone out of my pocket, I texted Sabrina.

Antonio: Where are you?

Sabrina: Lunch meeting, babe.

Antonio: Who are you with?

Sabrina: Why?

Antonio: This isn't the time to defy me.

Sabrina: *This isn't the time to question me. I'm working, simple as that.*

Growing impatient with her attitude, I glanced up at the entire room of guys staring at me in amusement.

"Fuck off."

"Little brother, you got it bad."

"Whatever, Bruno. I need to find Sabrina. Carlo, let's take a ride. Sonny, text me her location."

"Sure thing, boss," Bruno joked.

CHAPTER EIGHTEEN

SABRINA

Sitting inside Gold Post Restaurant with Derrick had me on edge. After Antonio's text message, something about his tone just left me wondering if he had spies watching my every move.

"Sabrina, you seem distracted. Am I boring you?"

"Sorry, Derrick, what did you say?"

Taking a sip of my water, I cleared my throat and dabbed the sweat off my forehead with my napkin.

"Are you hot? We can go someplace else if you'd like."

"Sorry, my fian… I mean boyfriend just pissed me off and made me a little flustered."

"If you were my girlfriend, I'd have you smiling all the time."

"That's sweet, but we need to get back to business. Your company wants to invest in a few offshore accounts, correct?"

"Correct. I have the research paperwork of the companies that you asked me to bring."

"Perfect! I was thinking we spread the five million between—"

Seeing Antonio point a gun at Derrick's head made my stomach drop.

Glancing up at the restaurant, all the other guests stared at what was going on, and I felt completely guilty for not answering his question.

"Antonio, please put the gun down."

Noticing Derrick had a smirk on his face had me questioning his sanity. Anyone with a brain knew when you have a gun to your head, you pleaded for your life.

"I asked you one question, Bella, and again, you defy me. When are you going to learn that you belong to me?"

"Baby, this is a work meeting. Look, I promise he's a client of Washington Finance."

"Baby, you have five minutes to get up and go to my car. Carlo will escort you out and take you home."

"Antonio, this is ridiculous. I have a job, and I won't be bullied into dropping every male client because you're jealous.

"Is that what you think?"

"Yes, what other reason is there?"

"I see Derrick didn't tell you who he really is, huh?"

"Antonio, listen to your girlfriend. You don't want any accidents to happen."

Seeing him shoving the gun into Derrick's face, I jumped between Antonio and Derrick.

"Sabrina, if you value our relationship, you'll leave and not question me."

"Just tell me what he did to you or our relationship, Tony."

The restaurant manager spoke with the waitress, and they both walked over to our table.

"Mrs. Washington, I need for you and your guests to leave. We can't have this kind of disturbance in our establishment."

"I apologize, Marco."

I placed my hand on top of Antonio's, forcing him to look into my eyes.

"Please, for me, put the gun away, and we can talk about this when I get home."

Narrowing his eyes at me, then shifting his weight from right to left, he motioned for Sonny and Bruno to grab me.

"Let go of me, Bruno!"

"Sorry, Sabrina, we take orders from Capo only."

"Antonio, I swear if you do anything to him, I won't be home when you get there. I'm done with this macho caveman bullshit."

Clenching his fist and scanning the crowd, he decided to pass the gun to Carlo. Twisting out of Sonny and Bruno's arms as Antonio walked closer to me, I looked over at Carlo holding the gun to Derrick's head.

"Don't ever threaten me, Bella. You won't like my punishment. I'll walk you out, and we can talk on the way home."

Snatching out of his grasp, I ignored his threat.

"Sonny, take me back to work."

"Boss."

"You may listen to him; I don't. You can either take me back, or I'll find another way… and don't look at him."

"Take her back to the office, Sonny, and stay there, even if you have to sit outside her office."

Passing me my purse, I yanked it out of Bruno's hand and stomped toward my car.

"See you later for dinner, baby!" Antonio yelled.

Giving Antonio the middle finger, I slid into the passenger seat and slammed the door.

"What do you want to do with him?"

"We should give our visitor a tour of New York. I have the perfect place to start with."

"She's right about one thing, Antonio…" Carlo stated.

"I suggest you worry about your situation with Janice before you comment on my Bella."

"You need to control your jealousy a little better, brother."

Thinking over Carlo's statement, I walked up to Bruno, holding onto Derrick's arm with the gun pointed at his side.

"I could have sworn I told you to stay away from her, Detective."

His eyes glinted with amusement.

"Capo De Luca finally shows up. I didn't think you'd have the balls to do it in open public."

"That's your misstep right there, Mr. Smith."

"What is?"

"Underestimating the extent of my power. You fooled my fiancée into thinking you're some legit businessman and probably thought you could get a date in as well."

"It was her idea for this lunch date. I just suggested the location."

"Yeah, a location that's near De Luca territory. Did you think I wouldn't admit my family's ties?"

"We both know you're not crazy enough to do anything to an DEA agent. Let me go, and I'll look into giving you a plea deal if you turn over everything you know about the other families."

"Mr. Smith, you're not very smart for an agent. I could care less about some deal or anything else concerning the police. What we have is called a miscommunication, and the only way to solve it is to make it go away."

"What does that mean?"

"Don't worry, I'll make sure to send your wife and kids a lovely flower arrangement for the funeral. Yellow is still her favorite color, right?"

Pushing him into the car, I headed over to Carlo's Mercedes, and we drove to the warehouse.

CHAPTER NINETEEN

SABRINA

"Sabrina, meet me in my office and bring Janice with you," Dad said as he poked his head into my office and walked back out.

I looked up from my cell phone, while returning a message to Antonio.

"Yes, sir."

Catching Janice walking past my door, I entwined arms with her, and we huddled up in conversation.

"What's up, Donna?"

"Girl, don't call me that mess. You sound like Antonio's crazy ass."

"Shit, I don't think anyone is crazier than he is, and that's something coming from me. You know in school, they diagnosed me a little off."

"Shut up, Janice. You are not slow. Just highly emotional in certain situations."

"Bitch, if you call setting your boyfriend's house on fire, running him off the road, and putting laxatives in his food because you thought he was cheating and come to find out he was just planning a surprise party for you, I'd think they would call you crazy."

We both burst into laughter at her description of her high school romance.

"Oh my God! Janice, I still can't believe you did those things. Speaking of, have you heard from Trevor lately?"

Walking into the conference room, we sat next to each other.

"Actually, he tried to reach out to me over the past few weeks, and I've ignored his texts."

Pouring a glass of water, we waited for my father to come into the room.

"How long has it been since you've spoken with him?"

Passing her a glass of water, she waved me off and checked her phone for any messages.

"You remember how we ended, and I thought it was best for us to move on after the situation."

"You guys were high school and college sweethearts. I think you need closure. Probably why he's calling you now, but I know I'm the last person to give love advice."

"Last thing I need is another man in my life. And why are you trying to give me love advice? Child, you can barely be in the same room with your baby daddy."

"I've specifically asked you to call him the father of my child. I hate when people say baby daddy."

"Did you suck his penis? Sleep with him without using protection and have a child with this man?

"Yes…" I mumbled.

"Repeat that louder please?"

"I said yes!"

"Well, I guess that makes him a baby daddy."

"I question our friendship a lot more lately."

"Really? You should have been questioning why you keep opening your legs to Antonio."

"Bitch, 'cause he's fine."

Bursting into laughter, we stopped talking once my father entered the room and closed the door.

"I see you both are having fun today when our company could be in the midst of a crisis," Father said.

"What are you talking about? What crisis?"

Passing me a memo sheet, I glanced at Janice, and she shrugged her shoulders, unaware of what was happening. Reading through the forms, I saw several showing Spencer's name on a warrant affidavit for a federal case dealing with the laundering of funds from our company.

"If I wasn't so pissed at your boyfriend for breaking your heart and this whole kidnapping situation, I would have him kill Spencer again for me."

"How did you know about Antonio killing Spencer?"

"Um, do we really want to talk about somebody getting killed in this office? The walls are fragile."

My father leaned back in his chair and narrowed his eyes at me.

"Sabrina, I may be your father but at one point in time, I did run the streets. I know all about the De Luca Family, and I don't approve of your choice in men. But I know he loves you and my grandson deeply."

"Dad..."

"No, let me finish. When you came to our house for dinner, we had just found out about the situation with Spencer... then Antonio taking over the family and you just returning home. Your mother and I have been through the ringer emotionally, and I wanted to protect you. Again, he wouldn't be my first choice. Overall, I know he'll protect you at all costs," Dad explained.

"I appreciate that, but what are we going to do about the FBI wanting to look at our files and Spencer being dead?"

"I called our attorney today, and he's pulling all our

files. The biggest issue is the FBI finding out we have Antonio De Luca as a client. That's the easiest way for them to get him on any charges, if Spencer did anything illegal for him as a client."

"Antonio is a lot of things, but he wouldn't jeopardize the club business. I know that contract came from a Ryde investment with a liquor company."

"Well, I need you girls to pull everything he had on Antonio and the investments for Ryde. The quicker we can separate ourselves, the better."

"Are you dropping him as a client?"

"I agree with Sabrina, Mr. Washington. That may look suspicious… right before you hand over paperwork on money laundering, you drop the head of the De Luca crime family as a client," Janice pointed out.

Watching him head toward the door, he paused and turned around, facing us.

"First priority is looking into Spencer's files. After that, we'll let the attorneys handle it. Are we keeping AJ tonight? You know your mother can't go a day without either seeing or hearing him scream through the night."

"I'll try to stop by if I don't leave here too late."

He left the room leaving Janice and I alone. I picked up my phone to text Antonio.

Sabrina: Can you drop AJ off at my parents' tonight?

Antonio: No

Sabrina: Antonio, this is ridiculous. It was just a business lunch.

Antonio: We'll discuss this later.

Rolling my eyes in aggravation at his response, I put my phone away and looked through the paperwork on Antonio that Spencer oversaw.

CHAPTER TWENTY

ANTONIO

As the van pulled up to the warehouse, I turned my phone off, so I wasn't disturbed. Dealing with Sabrina and her back and forth with our relationship pissed me off. If she thought we were done, I'd show her the real Don of the De Luca Cartel. No one would keep us apart again, including herself.

"Get my gloves and mask."

Carlo stood beside me and placed my tools on the table.

"Are you sure about this?" Bruno asked.

"Let that be the last time you question me."

Sonny and Lenny placed Derrick in the middle of the floor with his hands tied behind his back and duct tape over his mouth.

"Let him speak. I'd prefer to hear his last words before I kill him."

Sonny bent down and snatched the tape off Derrick's mouth.

"Arghh. You need to let me go."

"Do you hear that, little brother? Detective Smith here wants us to let him go."

"Detective Smith, or would you prefer Derrick?"

Grabbing the crowbar off the table, I moved toward Derrick and smiled.

"I asked you to leave her alone, and what did you do? Huh…"

"Answer him."

"Ask Sabrina if I can taste it again?"

I laughed at his attempt to manipulate me. Raising the crowbar, I hit him across the back.

"Arghhh…"

Letting my men beat on Derrick for a few minutes, I turned around to pull my phone out of my pocket to check my messages. Noticing that everyone stopped moving, I glanced at Sabrina standing in the middle of my warehouse with a gun pointed at my men.

CHAPTER TWENTY-ONE

SABRINA

*L*iz parked the car and turned the lights off. After my argument at the restaurant earlier, I decided to do some investigating of my own. Learning about the De Luca Family had been eye opening and knowing we had a child together had me even more concerned.

"I can't believe you made me do this, Janice."

"What are you talking about, Sabrina?"

"I'm talking about us three, sitting in this car outside of a warehouse, stalking our boyfriends."

"Honey, I hate to break it to you, but Liz and I have a boyfriend. You have a situation that we like to call All The Days of Sabrina and Antonio's lives."

All three of us burst into laughter at her comment. Even though our situation was complicated and frustrating at times, I wouldn't trade any of it for the world.

"Are you sure about this, Sabrina?"

"No, but I need to find out what he's doing. You should have seen him when he crashed my meeting with Derrick earlier today."

Noticing Janice rolling her eyes at my statement, I waved her off and noticed more cars pulling in near the loading area.

"Don't piss me off with your little slick comments, Janice."

"Girl, you have to get over blaming him for your kidnapping. At the end of the day, he's your baby's daddy, and a fine one at that."

"Are you done?"

"See, that little attitude may work on Antonio. I'm your friend, and I'll always keep it real with you, straight up no chaser. You pushing him away is only hurting AJ and yourself at the end of the day. He's human, Sabrina, just like you and me."

"She's right, Sabrina, and you know we rarely agree on things that have to do with men," Liz agreed.

Focusing my attention back to the warehouse, we watched as more men in black suits pulled Derrick out of the car.

"Oh, my God. He kidnapped him."

"Damn, girl, is your pussy gold or what? Got this man out here kidnapping and killing anyone who looks your way."

Shaking in disbelief, I jumped out of the car and walked toward the entrance.

I moved slowly, hearing Janice and Liz whispering for me to slow down. We snuck around back to find a way inside. Seeing a broken window, we climbed through it and snuck over to the opened door of the room. Peering around the room and seeing a dozen men standing around holding guns and pointing them at Derrick, I decided to step out and try to save Derrick from further pain.

"Do you know who I am, Mr. Smith?" Antonio asked.

Watching Antonio with his dress shirt off and wearing

a white t-shirt with bloodstains had my mind in a state of confusion. My thoughts ranged from wanting to fuck him for looking so good, to kicking his ass for being so jealous and possessive.

"Antonio, don't be stupid. We both know you're not going to kill me," Derrick groaned out.

"Do we, Mr. Smith?"

Opening the door wider, I pulled the small handgun out of my back pocket and pointed it at Antonio.

"Stop this, Antonio!" I shouted.

Everyone in the room turned toward me and pointed their guns. The room fell silent as Janice and Liz tried to calm me down. I couldn't tell if Antonio was disappointed or turned on by me being here with a gun pointed at him.

"Bella, I knew you had it in you. I must say I didn't think the tables would be turned like this, with you pointing a gun at me."

"Antonio, call off your men and let Derrick go. We can talk about this at home. He's just a client at my job. I would never cheat on you."

"For the record, Antonio or Don, I didn't know she had that gun with her. So, if you could spare me, that would be great, and Carlo, the next time you leave me horny to come play bad guy, at least let me get a taste first," Janice said.

Turning my glare toward Janice, I pinned her with the meanest look of "Bitch, you tried it?"

"What?" Janice questioned.

"I think everyone should put down their weapons and talk like adults," Liz suggested.

Antonio came up closer, and I shook my head for him to stay back. He ignored me as he walked right into the gun.

"Get that gun out of my men's faces and take your ass home. I could give a shit about you working with that piece of shit. He's a fucking DEA agent, Bella. He played you, and your ass is up here holding a gun at me, defending this deceitful lowlife."

Sneering at Derrick, I lowered the gun.

"Now say goodbye to your little friend."

Antonio pulled a gun out from behind him and shot Derrick between the eyes.

"Hold up... No!" I screamed.

Turning my back to Derrick's dead body, Janice and Liz wrapped their arms around me.

"Sabrina."

Janice and Liz continued to comfort me as I cried over witnessing his death.

"Never question me again, Sabrina. You won't like it," Antonio said.

I headed out of the warehouse with Janice and Liz behind me.

CHAPTER TWENTY-TWO

SABRINA

Staying back in my old apartment, trying to make sense of the last year and a half of my life, I needed time to think without all the distractions of family, friends, and men, namely Antonio. He came into my world like a tornado, fast and furious, taking anything he wanted, without any regards to whose life he would destroy in the process. A part of me loved him with all my heart. The passion, love, and care he brought to the world, opened me up in ways I never imagined possible.

His jealousy and possessiveness got out of hand sometimes, but I overlooked it for what good he had in his heart. Looking down at AJ sleeping in his crib, I knew I couldn't keep his lifestyle from our son. He was the head of a mob cartel. He literally could have someone killed with the point of a finger.

"This isn't a life for you, AJ, or me. I wanted the white picket fence. Two kids, one dog, a husband who worked at a bank. Where the hell did I go wrong?" I thought somberly.

The doorbell rang. I looked over at the time, noticing it

was almost eight p.m. I got out of bed and grabbed the robe hanging on my chair.

The doorbell went off again, and I rushed to answer so it didn't wake up AJ.

"Who is it?" I asked.

Covering the peephole with his entire hand, Antonio waited for me to say something smart.

"If you don't answer, the door stays shut," I snapped angrily.

"It's me, baby," Antonio answered.

I wasn't feeling up to a confrontation. Thinking over the past year and a half when I met Antonio, fought his ex-girlfriend, had a child, got kidnapped, fought with his father... was this a healthy relationship for us to stay involved in?

"I need space, Antonio," I replied softly, hoping he understood.

Not giving up, Antonio knocked again.

"We can make this work, Bella," Antonio told me through the door.

"This is too much for me and AJ."

At the mention of his son's name, Antonio banged on the door louder.

"Either you open this door now, or I shoot my way inside. The choice is yours," Antonio demanded angrily.

"This is my home. We agreed for me to have space. I'll call the police if you don't leave. Think about our son."

I heard silence for a few minutes, then mumbling. Suddenly, I heard a drill on the other side of the door.

"You can't be serious right now. Antonio, if you bust down my door, I'll kick your ass. Don't let the red bottoms and cute face fool you. I dare you to break my door down."

Getting aroused by my attitude and wanting to see me in person, Antonio banged on the door again.

"Open the door, or the drill is next," Antonio demanded through gritted teeth.

Believing he would knock it down, I unlocked the deadbolts and opened the door. Looking him in the eye, I could see he hadn't slept or eaten. He had bags under his eyes, and his hair grew out from not getting his weekly haircut.

"Happy now," I muttered as I walked off to check on AJ. Opening his door and seeing him knocked out in his crib, I felt relief that he didn't wake up at the noise. I came back to the living room and stood facing Antonio. He grabbed me up and tossed me over his shoulder. He spanked my right butt cheek twice and rubbed over the pain to soothe the stinging.

"Let me down, you psycho," I demanded.

Walking to the bedroom with me still over his shoulder. I beat him on his back, hoping he'd let me down.

"I don't belong to you. Dammnit, Tony, please let me down."

Pushing the door of my bedroom open further, he noticed his son sleeping peacefully.

Rather than move AJ, he took me to the guest bedroom. Locking the door and placing me on my feet, I smacked him in the face.

"Get the fuck out of my house. You pull this shit and think I'll be with you."

Seeing that I was getting ready to smack him again, Antonio grabbed my hand, seething mad from the pain of the first hit. He pulled me over to the bed. Sitting down, he tossed me over his legs.

"What are you doing? I know damn well you aren't about to spank me."

"Are you going to calm down so we can talk like adults?" Antonio asked.

Squirming in his lap, I stopped fighting and decided to let him win this round.

"Fine, go ahead and say what you need to say, then leave."

"I'm not leaving until after we talk."

Taking his shoes off, pulling off his jacket, and placing his gun on the nightstand, Antonio sat back down and pat the bed for me to join him.

"I didn't agree to any space. You wanted space, I said no," Antonio said.

I tried to interrupt, but he cut me off. Pointing to the both of us, he continued his statement.

"We love each other. Yes, we've had some battles to conquer. But that doesn't mean give up. You belong to me. I told you that the first time we met," Antonio reminded me.

Rolling my eyes and looking away from him, I ignored the heat rising between my legs.

"I can smell your arousal, baby. I know you want me just as much as I want you. Stop running and believe in us. This will never end. I don't care how much you run, or try to say we're too different. There's one thing you'll never do," Antonio boasted.

"What's that?"

"Make me believe that we don't belong together. Baby, you're my peace in this crazy world. My heart was cold until you came, and I can't go back to that place before you, especially with you giving me a child. AJ and you are the best things that's ever happened to me," Antonio muttered.

Antonio looked into my eyes and smiled. I looked off sadly.

"Why do you look so sad? I'm here fighting for us. Isn't that what you wanted?" Antonio demanded.

I got off the bed and went to the window. Looking out at the sky, I contemplated telling Antonio about my time in Italy with Alex.

"Do you hate me?"

Antonio stood up from the bed, walked up behind me, and wrapped his arms around my waist.

"Why would you ask me something like that? Baby, I love you," Antonio answered.

"I hated you. I know it's crazy, but I blamed you for me being kidnapped, finding you with Camilla, thinking you got back together with her, and then getting pregnant."

Antonio rubbed his hand up and down my shoulder, comforting and soothing the hurt and pain that had crept its way into my voice.

"I know. You have every right to feel that way. I don't hate you for not telling me about my little bambino. You had your reasons. We have to forgive to move forward. All my enemies are being taken care of as we speak. I swear to never let anything hurt you or AJ," Antonio promised.

"You can't promise that, Tony. This life you lead comes with so much responsibility. I wouldn't want you to feel like you had to choose."

I turned around and placed my hands on Antonio's cheeks.

"Sabrina, I refuse to live without you and my son. If I have to lock you up, then I will," Antonio bellowed.

I shook my head in disbelief at his aggressiveness. Turning away from him and sitting, I kicked off my house shoes.

"I have a few demands. If this is going to work, then you have to agree to my list."

Antonio agreed and kissed my lips.

"Not so fast, player. Before the loving, I need my terms met," Sabrina grumbled.

"Of course, baby. What would you like?" Antonio sat with a smug expression on his sexy face.

"First off, you slowly retire from the cartel world. Second—"

Antonio interrupted with a shake of his head in agreement.

"I need verbal and written confirmation, sir."

Antonio licked his lips and kissed me.

"I like it when you call me sir. I'll sign anything," Antonio answered.

"Focus please. Second, I don't want your father anywhere near my son. Your mother is fine; Jimmy cannot see our child until he gets over his bigotry. I won't budge on that and if you feel it's not something you can handle, then please leave my home, because we can work out visitation through the courts," I boasted.

A spark of anger washed across Antonio's face at the mention of courts and custody battles.

"Sabrina, I tolerate a lot of things, but you need to understand something. I'm a man, and no one runs me. Not my father, you, the cartel, or the courts. No one will tell me what I can do with my son or when I can see him. Do you understand me?" Antonio demanded.

Staring Antonio in the eyes as he spoke, not wanting to look away first, I finally nodded in agreement.

"Now…" I told.

Antonio cut me off.

"No, I'm done with your demands. We are together, and that's it. No more outside people, friends, or family. Just Antonio and Sabrina, plus AJ. Got it?" Antonio asked.

"Got it."

"I have one more question for you," Antonio asked.

"What?" I yawned and lay on the bed.

Antonio pulled the ring out of his pants pocket and

dropped to his knees. Shocked and flustered by his surprise proposal, I almost passed out.

"Will you make me the happiest man in the world and marry me, Sabrina Washington?"

Tears fell down my cheeks at the surprise proposal. I was speechless.

"Yes… Antonio. Yes, I'll marry you."

CHAPTER TWENTY-THREE

ANTONIO

The chiming of the bells echoed throughout the church. I was wearing a black suit with white cufflinks. I watched as my mother tickled AJ, bouncing him on her knees the way she used to calm us down. Taking in these moments I'd only dreamed of ever since meeting Sabrina, I knew I was just a few minutes away from being her husband, and it made all the drama worthwhile. Finding out about my uncle's betrayal, my father still not agreeing with me marrying Sabrina and not showing up for our wedding or even acknowledging his grandchild hurt, but it wouldn't stop the love I had for Sabrina. There was nothing he could do to make me change my mind. Meeting her had made my life so complete and worthwhile.

The kind of love we'd experienced left me speechless most of the time. Other times, her stubbornness, headstrong personality, even her controlling nature, had gotten on my nerves. Her love, laugh, and spirit had outweighed them all.

"I need to talk to her," I said to myself aloud.

Mom frowned up at my suggestion.

"Tony, you'll see her in a few minutes at the altar. Baby, please be patient," Mom answered.

I couldn't sit still. I needed a few minutes alone without all the distractions. Just being in her presence would allow my nerves to calm down.

"At least let me talk to her, I need to make sure she's okay."

Carlo was on the phone with Janice, trying to intervene.

"Babe, is Sabrina dressed yet?" Carlo asked.

"Why, you aren't marrying her," Janice inquired, sarcastically.

"Calm down, woman. I'm asking for Antonio. You keep up this attitude, you know what'll happen," Carlo murmured lowly.

Mom laughed at Carlo on the phone with Janice bickering.

"Are those two always like this?" Mom asked.

I picked AJ up from my mother's lap. He was the ring bearer even though he kept trying to eat the ring. He matched me in a black tailored suit, wearing a necklace with the inscriptions of AJ on the bottom. I kissed his cheek and walked out of the room.

"I'll be back," I told everyone in the room.

"That boy never listens. Just imagine when he gets married," Mom mumbled.

Carlo and Mom followed behind AJ and me.

We all walked toward Sabrina's room and heard Janice's loud mouth through the door. Even with the door slightly closed, I saw through the outside window, Sabrina standing in the mirror in a long mermaid dress with the back cut out. A long veil covered her face, a wedding gift from Liz. She also wore her mom's earrings from her wedding and a blue garter belt from Janice. Since being with me, she decided that once we got settled, she wanted to convert from Baptist to Catholic. I knew she was making a sacrifice, and the process was over a year long. As long as she was mine with my last name, that was all that mattered to me.

"This is the last time I get you a wedding gift. You better make this stick and no more running away," Janice bellowed.

"Girl, hush. I'm dressed, aren't I? Liz, please get your friend. I have no time for her today."

"You can boss your man around, but bitch, not me. Issa fight a bride heifer," Janice joked.

Listening to the laughter from outside the room, Carlo and my mom chuckled at the friendship they had.

Knocking on the door, it got quiet on the other side.

"Were you expecting someone?" Liz asked.

"No. Maybe it's my mom," Sabrina answered.

"Ohh… shit, I forgot… it's Antonio," Janice replied.

"What! He can't see me before the wedding, it's bad luck."

"Baby, open up. I just want to see you for a minute. I need to see you."

"We only have a few minutes before the ceremony, baby. Can't you wait for me?"

"See, this is what good pussy do to you. Have him drunk off that love," Janice joked.

Liz and Janice laughed at Sabrina, trying to shut them up.

"Janice, my dear, we're in a church. Can you keep that language on the low as you young folks like to say," Mom scolded her.

All laughing stopped at Mom's talking.

"I know how to get her to shut up without having to…" Carlo offered.

"If you say what I think you're going to say, I'll slap you silly, Carlo Russo Jr. You're not too big for a whipping," Mom responded.

Carlo looked embarrassed at Mom chastising him in front of everyone.

I tried to open the door. Finding it locked, I knocked again.

"Baby, AJ needs changing. We both miss you, sweetheart," I said pleadingly.

"Girl, let me open this door before he kicks it down," Janice told her.

"Fine. Antonio, don't look at me. Turn around and talk."

"Fine, but I want to touch you. Grab my hand," I answered.

Sabrina watched through the peephole as I turned around with my back to the door. She opened the door and grabbed my hand from the back.

"What's going on, Tony? Are you having second thoughts?" Sabrina asked.

"Hell no, you belong to me. I just needed to see you and make sure this is real. We've gone through a lot, and sometimes, things don't head in the right direction. I feel at this moment, we've come full circle."

Mom took AJ out of my arms and walked into the room with Liz and Janice. Carlo stepped away to give them a few moments of privacy.

"Yes, we have, and I know deep down, that nothing can stop us, not your father, Camilla, Alex, or myself," Sabrina choked up.

"Baby, that's the past. We both agreed no more running for either of us. Let the past go and look toward the future. Now that you've given me a son, you'll never be able to get rid of me. I'm filling you up with more babies tonight."

Sabrina blushed at my mom hearing me talk about our sex life.

"Really, Tony, did you forget your mom's in the room?" Sabrina scolded.

Mom ignored my boasting and took AJ to the bathroom to change his diaper.

I smacked Sabrina on the ass and rubbed it to soothe the pain.

"Ouch, you asshole," Sabrina whined.

"Shut up. Just wait till I get you in my bed tonight." I grinned at what I had planned for our wedding night.

Sabrina smiled at the thought.

The church music started, and the wedding coordinator walked over to the bridal door.

"It's time, you guys," the bridal coordinator announced.

I squeezed Sabrina's hand.

"I'm right behind you, baby," Sabrina told him.

Carlo and I walked alongside the wedding coordinator as Janice passed Sabrina her flowers.

"My boo getting married. Now we can't hang out anymore," Janice whined.

"I'm just getting married. Antonio doesn't run anything over here. If I want to go out, then I will. Better recognize. I've always been Sabrina Washington, just adding De Luca to the last name. My self is still here." Sabrina chuckled.

"See, this is why she's my bitch. Yes, Queen," Janice gloated.

All guests stood as the music played for the bride to come down the aisle. The doors opened, and I met Sabrina's eyes. Both of us looked at each other with intense eye contact. Neither could move away from the other. I started to walk toward her, but Carlo had to pull me back.

"She's not going anywhere, bro. Chill out," Carlo told me.

Everyone in the church giggled at my eagerness to marry Sabrina.

Finally arriving at the altar, her father passed her hand into mine as he answered the preacher's question.

"Who gives this woman away?" the pastor asked.

"I do," Jonathan answered.

Jonathan pulled Sabrina into a tender embrace, kissed her forehead, and wiped a tear from his eyes.

"I love you, sweetheart," Jonathan told Sabrina.

"I love you too, Dad," Sabrina answered.

Jonathan shook hands with me and walked over to stand next to his wife.

Sabrina passed her bouquet of flowers to Liz, and I grabbed her hands. I kissed each hand and pulled her veil away from her face. I started to go in for a kiss on her lips, but the pastor stopped me.

"That's usually done at the end, Antonio," Father Joseph whispered toward Antonio.

Sabrina giggled and blushed at my eagerness.

"Baby, you have to wait for him to announce us," Sabrina said.

"I can't wait that long. Baby, you look so beautiful. I need to taste you," I muttered.

Sabrina placed her hand against my lips to shut me up before I said something inappropriate in a church.

"Sorry. My bad, Pastor. Go ahead."

After fifteen minutes of the service, they finally got to the end and the best part.

"I now pronounce you Mr. and Mrs. Antonio De Luca. You may kiss your bride," Father Joseph announced.

Everyone in the church clapped and screamed in joy for

Sabrina and me. Running my hand down her cheek, I smiled at the woman I claimed that very night in Ryde. She tried running away, but I found her every time. Now we were husband and wife.

"With pleasure," I groaned, sexily.

CHAPTER TWENTY-FOUR

SABRINA &ANTONIO

I walked into our bedroom with a tray carrying breakfast. After the wedding and two-week honeymoon, I was still in disbelief that I was now Mrs. De Luca. It would take some getting used to. After ending my engagement with Alex and my kidnapping, I didn't think I'd ever have happiness again.

Antonio was determined to get me back, and I tried breaking up with him again. He just told me if I tried running away again, he would find me and lock me up in his home. He didn't care about his father not liking me, or what anyone else thought. I was his woman, and that was all that mattered.

Placing the tray down, I admired my husband lying in bed with the sheets covering the bottom half of his body. His broad shoulders peeked out, while his chest rose and fell from his light snoring. Slowly climbing on the bed and pulling the covers over my head, I crawled between his legs and loved seeing my next best friend, his long, thick penis, lying against his leg. A wicked smile crossed my face.

I licked my lips while slowly stroking his dick. He didn't even make a sound.

"Someone's in a deep sleep," I mumbled to myself in amusement.

Bending down low and placing my mouth on his tip, his eyes popped open.

"Ahhh…Bella," he half-groaned.

I sucked more of his penis in my mouth and steadily built a pace. Watching him come undone was another favorite pastime of mine. I loved having this much control over him.

"Fuckkkk… Baby, wait," Antonio growled underneath his breath.

As I sped up the pace, he placed his hand on my hair and massaged my scalp. Out of habit, he thrust his hips faster and faster while fucking my throat.

"Arghhh… Sabrina!" Antonio yelled out.

Sucking up the last drop of his cum, Antonio watched me through hazy eyes as he tried to catch his breath. I went to get out of bed to brush my teeth, but he pulled me close to his chest, looking deeply into my eyes.

"You are amazing," Antonio panted weakly, slowly getting his breathing under control.

Leaning in, he captured my parted lips with his tongue and kissed me deeply while running his hands up and down my arms and thighs. Before anything could get started, a knock at the door interrupted us.

"Go away," Antonio yelled harshly.

I chuckled at his outburst and pushed him back on the bed. He gently grabbed my arms to keep me from answering the door.

"Don't answer that. I need some pussy, baby," Antonio pleaded.

"You are insatiable. What if it's the nanny, and AJ needs us?"

Antonio blew out a breath and watched as I got out of bed wearing only a nightgown and grabbed a robe to cover up.

"Hide your little friend before I open the door. We don't want to scare anybody."

"Baby, now you know there's nothing little about me," Antonio replied.

Antonio winked as I blushed and walked toward the door.

Opening the door, I saw my sister holding AJ.

"Hey, sis. Did he wake you up?" I asked. She placed a kiss on his lips and cheek.

Antonio got out of bed and grabbed his robe. He walked over and pulled AJ from Ashley's arms.

"Little guy here was crying for his daddy. I thought you'd be up. I need to head out and catch my flight back home," Ashley replied.

Antonio played with AJ in his arms, tickling and blowing raspberry bubbles on his stomach.

"I'm going to miss you so much. I hate we didn't get to spend much time together."

Ashley and I looked on as Antonio lay with AJ in his arms and fed him his bottle.

"It's so strange to see the big bad Don of De Luca Cartel bottle feeding a baby," Ashley said jokingly

I agreed, staring at my two favorite men.

"Just think, I was worried about getting over Alex's bullshit, and now I'm married with a baby. Life has a funny way of changing you."

"So true. But anyway, let me get out of here. My car is waiting downstairs, and I still need to check in with Mom and Dad before my flight."

"Okay, sis. Call me once you make it back home. Love you."

Ashley and I kissed and hugged goodbye. I went back into the bedroom and lay next to Antonio and AJ.

"Thank you, baby."

I looked up at Antonio in wonder.

"Thank me for what?"

"For marrying me and giving me a son. I still can't believe Camilla and Alex were working together. I should have suspected something earlier. My focus was on Spencer and my brother too much."

I melted at his anguish of not being able to find me sooner. I rose off the bed and grabbed him by his chin.

"You have nothing to apologize for. None of us thought he would go off the deep end like that. It's over, and I'm fine. Now let's plan our day with our little bambini. Issa married woman now."

I leaned in and softly kissed Antonio on the lips and AJ on the forehead. I picked up the fork and continued eating breakfast and talking with Antonio. A few minutes later, after finally getting out of bed, Antonio finished feeding AJ and burped him.

"We should get the family together and have a barbeque. Your mom would love hanging with AJ today," I suggested.

Antonio looked sad as I brought up having a family get-together. I pulled clothes for Antonio and myself out of the closet.

"Cara... I can't today. I have a business meeting."

"Tony, you promised you'd retire from that life. I'm not putting up with that bullshit anymore."

"Just have one meeting today, and then Bruno along with Carlo will handle the illegal business end," Antonio answered.

Walking off to the bathroom in a huff, I slammed the bathroom door. AJ cried from the loud noise of the door slamming.

"Hey, little man. Daddy's got you."

Our son continued wailing as Antonio cradled him in his arms. He slowly calmed down and went back to sleep.

"That's a good boy," Antonio said.

Walking to the nursery and placing AJ back in his crib, Antonio covered him up and went back into our bedroom to try to smooth things over with me.

Hearing the water running for the shower, he decided to leave things as is and get his day started.

"She'll calm down later; a little time alone will help," Antonio mumbled to himself.

Twenty minutes later, Antonio was dressed from head to toe in a dark-blue suit, black tailored shoes, with a black and light blue tie. Grabbing his keys off the counter, he talked to Carlo as he was about to head out for the day. I walked down the stairs with AJ in my arms.

"I'll meet you at the warehouse in a few minutes. Just finishing up at home," Antonio told Carlo over the phone.

I rolled my eyes as Antonio looked at me when I walked by without acknowledging him. I moved away as he tried to kiss me on the lips. I walked over to the living room table and grabbed my purse and keys.

"She's fine. Stubborn as usual. Tell her that her friend needs to get her attitude in check before she gets a spanking." Antonio smirked and winked at me.

I pushed him off as he tried to grab my butt. He laughed and opened the door to let me walk out first.

"My wife isn't talking to me at the moment. Maybe we should double date," Antonio joked.

I glared over my shoulder at his joke and threw the middle finger up. As I opened the door to my Lexus SUV and strapped AJ in his seat, I walked around to the driver's side of my brand-new wedding present and got inside, pulling off and heading to my parents' house.

Antonio jumped inside his Porsche and drove off toward the cartel warehouse.

* * *

THREE HOURS LATER, family and friends gathered in the backyard of my parents' home, and I was surrounded with the people I loved the most, listening to music, barbequing, dancing, and drinking.

Liz held AJ in her lap. Dad was grilling steaks and showing my mom the latest techniques he'd learned.

Janice danced with me, showing me the latest moves.

"Girl, you better work that big booty you got," Janice joked.

Janice slapped my ass as I twerked to the music.

"My baby likes my big booty," I shouted teasingly.

"You ain't ever lied. Antonio will literally kill if someone even looks at you too long," Janice joked.

Liz and I nodded in agreement at her joke.

"At the moment, he can't even look at me with his dumb ass," I muttered sadly.

"Ohhh…Do I hear fighting already for the newlyweds? Tell Therapist Janice what's the tea," Janice inquired.

I went to sit next to Liz as Janice followed.

"We fought this morning," I said somberly.

"About what?" Liz asked

Janice passed a drink to me and pulled AJ out of my lap.

"Give me my godbaby. He is so sweet," Janice demanded.

I looked on at my parents kissing and hugging near the grill, wondering if I'd ever get to that place of peace. As I was about to explain the fight, Carlo and Bruno ran into the backyard, pushing people out of the way. The music stopped, and my friends and family looked on at Carlo screaming at me. My father started to approach, but my mom held him back.

"Sabrina, why the hell didn't you answer your phone?" Carlo demanded.

Carlo pulled my arm, shaking me in anger.

"Carlo, let her go!" Janice screamed.

"We've been looking for you for hours!" Carlo shouted aggressively. Dealing with last-minute unexpected work calls and a crying baby, I'd disappeared to handle things so our celebration wouldn't be interrupted.

As soon as Carlo ran in, I felt an immediate tightening in my chest. I knew this day would come soon. After the last shooting, my worries only intensified.

"What happened?"

I grabbed AJ and headed out of the backyard. I kissed my son as Carlo, Bruno, and Janice followed behind us.

"Where is he?"

"Sabrina, we need to talk privately. What needs to happen next is something that Antonio never wanted for you. Seeing as how we never thought we'd get to this place, we need to make some decisions," Carlo replied.

I stopped walking and turned toward Carlo.

"What are you talking about, Carlo?"

Carlo looked at Bruno in confirmation of what he was about to reveal. Bruno agreed with a head nod.

"Just spit it out."

"There was an explosion at the warehouse," Carlo replied.

I almost fainted at the news, while still holding AJ. Janice grabbed him out of my arms. Bruno held me up before I faltered again.

"We didn't know it was a trap. Some of the local bosses aren't happy with Antonio's choices lately," Carlo said.

"What choices are you talking about?"

"We need to get you to someplace safe," Carlo explained.

Carlo tried to pull me toward the passenger seat of his car. I refused to move.

"What choices, Carlo? And don't lie to me."

"You and him. The cartel, like his father, isn't the biggest fan of him being married to you," Carlo answered.

"You've got to be shitting me!" Janice yelled. I held my hand up to calm Janice down. "No. This is fucking 2018; these motherfuckers need to get over it. They wished they could get some of this black queen."

"Baby, I know how you feel. But right now, we need to focus on Sabrina and AJ," Carlo replied.

I placed my hand on AJ's right cheek and smiled as he looked at me and giggled.

"You look so much like your father. He would be so proud of you. We love you so much, AJ."

I leaned over and kissed his cheek. I smelled his scent, taking it into memory.

Pulling myself together, I looked at my friends and hugged both Liz and Janice.

"I love you guys so much."

"What are you going to do?" Liz inquired.

Passing Liz my baby bag and hugging Janice, I opened my purse and pulled out a gun. Checking the chamber and making sure it was still on safety, I placed it back in my purse.

"Doing what I need to do for my family. Take AJ to my parents. Tell them if I don't call in an hour, then they know what my wishes are for AJ."

"Sabrina, think this through. You can't go off and fight

in some war, trying to avenge his death. What about your condition?" Liz asked gently.

Everyone stopped talking and moving at hearing Liz bring up my condition. Had I told Antonio what was going on, maybe he'd still be here with me.

"Bruno, call a meeting with Jimmy. I want a face-to-face sit down. Get the other Dons to meet at Antonio's. I'm the Donna of this family. My husband may be missing or no longer with us, but I'm the head of this family now. Being pregnant won't stop what I'm about to unleash. You mess with my mine, then you get dealt with accordingly," I demanded angrily.

EPILOGUE

SABRINA

Five years later, Antonio and I were living in Italy with our three kids. We happily cheered on our oldest son AJ as he played soccer.

"Come on, AJ, you got this," I yelled in excitement.

AJ looked over at me, yelling and screaming. He then looked at his dad with a pleading to calm me down from embarrassing him.

"I'm sorry, buddy. It's in her blood," Antonio joked.

I slapped Antonio on his shoulder. I stood with my leg poked out to the side, hands on my ample hips, still thick from having three kids. I continued getting a workout in, even if Antonio didn't think I needed it. I stayed healthy before I even met him by staying fit and working out. With my upper lip turned into a frown, I thought about a way to get my husband back for trying to embarrass me for cheering on our baby boy. I didn't care how I looked. He was the firstborn, my little miracle baby.

Antonio admired my beauty. According to him, I still looked as gorgeous as the first time we met at Ryde. To this day, every year on our anniversary, we went back to Ryde

and reminisced about the first meeting, my stubborn attitude and his possessiveness from claiming me on the first
night.

I often laughed at his alpha personality that he carried
when we went out now. Even if it was the grocery store,
he made sure I was always protected, especially if the
kids were with me. Becoming the Donna of De Luca
Cartel was both a blessing and a curse. Not seeing my
family as often, except holidays or birthdays, left me sad
because I grew up in a close-knit family. I wanted the
same for our three kids. Looking over at the family that I
created with the love of my life made up for the short-
comings. Our three kids, AJ, Jonathan, named after my
father, and Isabella, the baby of the family, kept us on our
toes.

"Baby, I'm sorry, but you're embarrassing him," Antonio
joked.

Antonio pulled me into his arms, and I stubbornly
crossed my arms under my breasts to keep distance
between us. Antonio looked down at my five-foot-seven
frame and smirked at my unwillingness to hug him back.

He bit my right cheek.

"Ouch, that hurt, asshole."

Antonio gently kissed me on the right cheek that he bit.
Janice and Carlo walked over from the concession stand
with their two kids, followed by Liz and Bruno.

"Why don't you two get a room?" Janice told them
teasingly.

I rolled my eyes at Janice and waved her off. Antonio
bent down to kiss my lips.

"Give me a kiss, woman."

"I only kiss my husband."

Antonio smacked my ass, and I yelped from the pain.

"Don't get your ass spanked out here. You know I'll take

you to the bathroom and give you something to tighten up that attitude. Now give me a kiss," Antonio told me.

I huffed out a breath, stood on my tippy toes, and kissed Antonio on the lips. He smiled, and I smiled back at him, no longer mad.

"You already got three kids. If you keep that up, you'll end up with two more," Liz said.

Bruno sat next to Liz and pulled her onto his lap.

"Little brother, did you talk with Pops today?" Bruno asked.

"Bruno, we said no business today," Liz muttered.

Bruno kissed her shoulder and nodded in agreement.

"He said to call him later. He was getting ready to travel with Mom out of the country again. Ever since he retired, she's kept him busy," Antonio replied.

"How is your dad doing since you've married Sabrina and had kids?" Janice asked.

"Janice, stay out of their business. Worry about your own family," Carlo demanded.

Janice ignored Carlo and pulled me out of Antonio's grip. For a few minutes, they played tug of war. He didn't want to let me go.

"Damn, Tony, I'll bring her right back. Geeezzzz," Janice said, annoyed.

I laughed at the exchange and kissed him again on the lips to calm his temper down.

"Baby, go hang with your friends. I'm right here. Besides, this section is about to get lit up with screaming for our baby boy."

As they continued talking, AJ scored another goal. The entire family and crowd erupted in cheers.

Antonio admired his son playing on the field. Our two kids, Jonathan and Isabella sat next to him, eating their popcorn and cheering for their brother. He looked across the bench and caught me staring back at him at the same time. I smiled and mouthed, "I love you."

He mouthed, "I love you too." When the game was over, while walking back toward our cars, his phone rang. He passed to me Isabella and Jonathan's bag. AJ helped Isabella get into the car as I helped Jonathan.

"This better be important," Antonio asked.

Sonny Demarko, one of the cartel's hit men, was on the other end of the line.

"Sorry, Capo, we have a situation that came up. We need your help," Sonny asked.

"You know my brother handles most of the deals now," Antonio said.

"I understand, but this isn't business related," Sonny replied.

Antonio tensed up at the meaning of his words. Only other thing in this world he was willing to die for was his family.

"What is it?" I ask.

"The Donna is being requested for a sit down," Sonny answered.

"Everyone knows she's not involved in my business," Antonio asked loudly.

I heard Antonio getting loud over the phone and walked toward him to try to calm his temper down.

"Babe, what's wrong?"

Antonio looked down at me with a frown on his face.

"She set a deal up after covering up your involvement in Camilla's death and killing Alex. The Riccis aren't too happy with her," Sonny informed.

Antonio looked wide eyed at me from what he was just heard. He knew I'd do anything to make sure his hands were clean of anything to do with Camilla Ricci. It had been six years since the kidnapping. They should've moved on since then.

"Let him know I'll be in touch," Antonio replied.

He abruptly hung up the phone. I noticed the silence from Antonio and the death glare he gave me. I figured he just found out about the side deals running the cartel behind his back.

"How long?" Antonio asked.

"About two years now. I knew you said you handled her, but I needed to make sure nothing came back on the family. Alex and Camilla took me away from you for over a year. You missed the birth of our baby because of that bitch," I explained.

"Okay, Mrs. De Luca," Antonio replied sweetly.

He pulled me into his arms, kissed my lips, both cheeks, and forehead softly.

"Are you mad?" I asked.

"The first time I saw you in my club, I knew you were made for me. You bring me peace. I need you to leave the cartel business to me. I don't need the fellas thinking you run things," Antonio answered.

Antonio softly caressed my butt cheek and squeezed. I wrapped my arms around his neck and kissed his cheek, then left ear.

"Ummm... I never can get enough," I moaned.

"You keep that up, and we will have another baby," Antonio groaned.

"Too late. I already confirmed with the doctor last week," I informed my shell-shocked husband.

Antonio pulled away from me and looked at me in disbelief. I was blushing and smiling in excitement.

I nodded in confirmation. Antonio picked me up and hugged me tightly, spinning us around near the car as the rest of the family looked on.

* * *

I HOPE you enjoyed Antonio and Sabrina's story. If you want more "Mafia Romance, why not try *"Antonio and Sabrina Book 4" Click here* https://books2read.com/u/4NQyE9

Have you read *yet "Temptation?* That is a standalone contemporary, sports, curvy girl romance. Check it out here https://books2read.com/u/mle1Vv

Please also check out my *"Heart of Stone Series"* https://books2read.com/u/boWPAV with a host of characters intertwined.

I hope you enjoyed Antonio and Sabrina's story. Please also check out my **"Heart of Stone 1" here** https://book s2read.com/u/boWPAV with a host of characters intertwined.

Check out Mafia romance here *"Antonio and Sabrina Book 1"* https://books2read.com/u/4AxKLo

Please also check out my **Mutual Agreement** " https:// books2read.com/u/mgzzWX a steamy political romance.

Have you checked out **"She's All I Need"** click here https://books2read.com/u/49lkeW a sports, opposites attract romance.

"Heart of Stone Book 4" here https://books2read.- com/u/4NXyPG with a host of characters intertwined.

READING ORDER OF STRUCK IN LOVE UNIVERSE

Order of Reading

The Early Years-A Prequel Short Story
https://books2read.com/u/49Zjnw
Ruthless Struck In Love Book 1
https://books2read.com/u/4AxKLo
Savage Struck In Love Book 2
https://books2read.com/u/bpED6g
Beast Struck In Love Book 3
https://books2read.com/u/3LpgdJ
Janice and Carlo Captivated By His Love
https://books2read.com/u/b6je6M
Brutal Struck In Love Book 4
https://books2read.com/u/4NQyE9
Stolen-Fuertes Mafia Cartel Book 1
https://books2read.com/u/mvZlgV
Saved-Fuertes Mafia Cartel Book 2
https://books2read.com/u/4DWwLd
Redemption Struck In Love Book 5
https://books2read.com/u/b5kZ8O

Betrayal-Fuertes Mafia Cartel Book 3
https://books2read.com/u/4A5LGp

READING ORDER OF HEART OF STONE

Heart of Stone Book 1 Emery and Jackson
https://books2read.com/u/boWPAV
Heart of Stone Book 1.5
https://payhip.com/b/kWg7
Heart of Stone Book 2 Jordan and Damon
https://books2read.com/u/ba2OMx
Heart of Stone Book 3.5 Bottoms Up
https://payhip.com/b/HGP1
Heart of Stone Book 3 Angela and Brent
https://books2read.com/u/31rx9l
Heart of Stone Book 4 Jessica and Joseph
https://books2read.com/u/4NXyPG

INTRODUCTION OF 304 PUBLISHING COMPANY

We showcase authors writing African American, Interracial, Women's Fiction, Urban Romance, Erotic, and Contemporary Romance novels. Along with Thriller, Suspense, Poetry, Beauty, and Style Books. Thank you for taking the time out to visit. Join our mailing list to stay updated with new releases and blog posts.

Thank you so much for reading and if you enjoyed the crazy ride and decide to leave a review we'd truly appreciate the support.

SPOTIFY PLAYLIST

Antonio and Sabrina Struck In Love Series

1. Heather Headley- In My Mind
2. Love on the Brain –Rihanna
3. Cockiness –Rihanna
4. 7/11- Beyonce
5. Crazy In Love- Beyonce
6. Radioactive- Imagine Dragons
7. When We- Tank
8. Insecure- Jasmine Sullivan
9. Ain't Too Proud to Beg- The Temptations
10. You Keep Me Hanging On-The Supremes
11. Be Without You- Mary J Blige
12. Fire and Desire- Rick James & Teena Marie
13. I'd Rather Go Blind- Etta James
14. Make You Feel My Love- Adele
15. Lost Without U- Robin Thicke
16. Apologize- One Republic

WHAT'S NEXT?!

Want to know what happens next?

Follow me on website to catch the next release.

Reviews are the lifeblood of the publishing world. They're read, appreciated, and needed.

Please consider taking the time to leave a few words on your review platform of choice.

Sign up for updates and sneak peaks at the site below. www.chiquitadennie.com

CATALOG RELEASES

By Chiquita Dennie:
Temptation
The Early Years-A Prequel Short Story
Antonio & Sabrina: Struck in Love, Books 1, 2, 3,4
Janice & Carlo: Captivated by His Love
Heart of Stone, Book 1: Emery & Jackson
Heart of Stone, Book 1.5: Emery & Jackson, A Valentine's Day Short Story
Heart of Stone, Book 2: Jordan & Damon
Heart of Stone, Book 3: Angela & Brent
Heart of Stone, Book 3.5: Jessica & Joseph Bottoms Up
Joaquin Fuertes (The Fuertes Cartel Book 1)
Cocky Catcher (A Hero Club Novel)
Bossy Billionaire (A Hero Club Novel)
Love Shorts-A Collection of Short Stories
Joaquin Fuertes (The Fuertes Cartel Book 1)
Exposed (Salvation Society Novel)
Joaquin Fuertes (The Fuertes Cartel Book 2)
Refuel (A Driven World Novel)

Pressure (A Driven World Novel)
Antonio and Sabrina: Struck in Love 5

ABOUT THE AUTHOR

Chiquita Dennie is an author of Contemporary, Romantic Suspense, Erotic and Women's Fiction.

Chiquita lives in Los Angeles, CA. Before she started writing contemporary romance, she worked in the entertainment industry on notable TV shows such as the Dr Phil show, Tyra Banks show, American Idol, and Deal or No Deal. But her favorite job is the one she's now doing, full time writing romance.

A Best-Selling Author and Award-winning Filmmaker, her first short film "Invisible" was released in Summer 2017 and screened in multiple festivals and won for Best Short Film. She also hosts a podcast that showcases the latest in Beauty, Business and Community called "Moscato and Tea." Her debut release of Antonio and Sabrina Struck in Love has opened a new avenue of writing that she loves.

If you want to know when the next book will come out, please visit my website at http://www.chiquitadennie.com, where you can sign up to receive an email for my next release.

www.ingramcontent.com/pod-product-compliance
Lightning Source LLC
Chambersburg PA
CBHW011202190726
48286CB00009B/2884